CHLOROPHOBIA

AN ECO-HORROR ANTHOLOGY

Edited by A.R. Ward

Chlorophobia

An Eco-Horror Anthology

A Ghost Orchid Press Anthology

ISBN (paperback): 978-1-9196387-8-2

ISBN (e-book): 978-1-9196387-9-9

Cover design and book formatting by Claire Saag

Cover image © Cranach via Shutterstock

O Rose thou art sick.
The invisible worm,
That flies in the night
In the howling storm:

Has found out thy bed
Of crimson joy:
And his dark secret love
Does thy life destroy.

— *William Blake*,
"The Sick Rose"

CONTENTS

FOREWORD

What is eco-horror? Broadly speaking, eco-horror is any horror story with an ecological theme. Plants, animals, natural phenomena... It's about nature fighting back. There have long been horror stories about these themes—*Day of the Triffids,* anyone?—but in this age of intense anxiety about the impact humans are making on the planet Earth, it seemed like an incredibly timely and pertinent subgenre to highlight. Horror has a way of seeking out those niggling fears that get under our skin on a daily basis, and bringing those fears into the spotlight. That's what I wanted to do with this anthology.

All that said, I tried to avoid too much of a preaching tone with my selections. Yes, there are serious issues to discuss, but these authors manage to do so with creativity and a light touch. Because these stories and poems are short and snappy, there's likely to be something for all manner of horror fans here, whether you're into fast-paced, gory thrillers or lyrical, Gothic poetry.

But don't let me keep you any longer. Get reading, and I hope you enjoy discovering these new authors!

A.R. Ward

GROUNDING EXERCISE

Cormack Baldwin

Breathe in.

Thank you for taking this time to journey with us in grace. Take this moment to ground yourself in your heart place, wherever your physical body may be. Silence the clack of keys around you. Let the hum of the office fade. Let the tap of plastic heels against barren concrete melt away as you find yourself here.

Good.

With us, picture a grand forest, with a rushing brook and a soft carpet of moss. Hold this image, and imagine it receiving your love, your admiration, your very being, with open arms. You are at peace here. You belong here.

Breathe in the deep, rich aroma of the leaves rotting atop the forest floor. It's a smell you remember well, perhaps from vacations, perhaps from home. You remember crawling on your hands and knees through somewhere just like here, feeling water well up from the moss beneath your toes. It fills you up in a way you haven't felt in a long time.

Let us consider all our senses as we ground ourselves into this place. Open your eyes to the mottled green and gold of the forest. The branches overhead seem monochromatic at first, but look closer. Drink in the apricot light of dusk, only now filtering through the canopy. Rust-red bark peeks through velvety leaves and ends in delicate buds the color of seafoam.

Listen close. Empty your mind of the rush of thoughts and let the silence resolve into a thousand minute sounds—the distant snapping of twigs under an unsuspecting mammal's foot, the rapid beat of wings as a bird is flushed from its hiding place among the undergrowth. Closer, now, to the drones of insects pouring their hearts out to a lover who may not live to meet them. The subtle rustle of wind through leaves. All of these sing out at once. Grasp each song, hold it apart from the others. Tear the world apart until you can see the silver threads that hold it together, then watch it pull itself back together as one.

Rest your hand on the tree to your east—the one that stands above the rest, its aged gray bark forming a pillar that nearly blocks out the sun. Let the dirt and lichen that has accumulated over the millennia of its existence crumble against your palm. Run your thumb along each exquisite ridge and valley. You've never seen the top of this tree. You cannot so much as picture it. It feels wrong, somehow, as if to do so would render it inert. Yet it is there, and nature does not waste what the tree has provided. Far above you is a world you are not privy to. Breathe in and taste the humidity that is the only sign of what lies above. Breathe in the tang of sap where you pull your hand away. Let your mouth hang open like a wild cat's as it scents the air.

Now focus in on the feeling of life. The quiet hum in and around you. It is not sound, it cannot be separated into neat melodies and harmonies, nor cut and divided like colors. It's stronger here than you can remember it having ever been. It lies beneath you, in a web of hyphal network that allows mother trees to whisper the secrets of life to their decaying children. The roar of chainsaws mean nothing here. The trees will smuggle life to still-bleeding stumps, mock the lightning the sky threatens to call down on them. The ozone smell of storm, too, is alive, alive with crackles of electricity and heavy rain. Birds spread their wings under a dome of clouds, let the first raindrops speckle their feathers like stars.

Life is where you stand, too. It is in your every cell. It clutches your heart. For every concrete barrier you erect, you cannot forget that you are of the same world as the soft rot beneath your feet. Feel it undulate now, feel it pulse just out of step with your treacherous heart. You must keep time with this world. You have spent too long thinking you could peel yourself cleanly away, return at will, run the world at your pace.

There is no running any longer.

The steady of the thrum of the forest disappears, and for a moment the only things that remain are your heart beating in your chest and its faint echoes against the trees. Count each heartbeat as you breathe in against the stifling silence.

One.

Two.

Three.

Good.

Let the roar wash over you, shake you to your core just as it shakes the earth you stand on to that very spot. This is the sound of cataclysm. This is the sound of the earth breaking.

This is the sound of the end.

The earth rises around you, its coating of moss cracking under the wave of long-dead matter. Bones and blood are returned to the soil from which they rose, pulverized into indistinguishability from the black mat of rot. You will become one with it again, if only you can open yourself to it.

Feel it as earth, soft and rich, flows through your throat, tumbles down your lungs, and fills the branches of your airways with life, true life, not empty air. You will not be wasted here. Already, crawling things explore your nose and mouth, the soft skin of your underbelly and wrists. You will be used to grow, to raise a world of new life from where there was once only one.

The last molecules of hoarded air are displaced by the finest grains as the soil presses closer. Hear the hum of your heart and remember you are safe here. Feel your heart slow as your vision blurs to the color of the soil around you. This is where you are meant to be.

Breathe out.

CORMACK BALDWIN is very bad at meditation, and believe him, he's tried. He does, however, like forests, and thinks being digested by mushrooms doesn't sound too bad. If you would like to discuss being eaten by nature (or other things), say hi @cormackbaldwin on Twitter.

ON THE ALTAR
OF THE ANTHROPOCENE

Lindsay King-Miller

girls light candles on windowsills, burn
incense after midnight, cup matches
until they blister fingertips. Wildfire season
lasts all year. Smoke curls
down from the mountains like a tongue
over broken teeth.

We drink tap water cocktails
salt the rim with soot. Even in the desert
we built fires in a circle of stones.
It hurts to breathe, it hurts to hold your breath.
The dead bodies of trees
we climbed as children unfurl their black
and desiccated roots in our lungs.
When we fuck, we taste fuel.

Girls with air conditioning and white noise machines
close the shades and wait for snow
calibrate their body rhythms to the blue light of the television
menstruate algorithmically and eat
fruit out of season.

It's the rest of us who feel the pull
who sleep naked with the windows open
howl our throats to bleeding
at the carcinogen-haloed moon

Inside we are water, expanding
in heat, following the tidal pull of damage.
The horizon is a witch and we are familiars, called to her summoning fire.

Every night we lay our bodies
on the sacrificial stone.
Every morning we climb from a bed of ashes
lick the char from our lips
and go to work.

LINDSAY KING-MILLER is the author of Ask a Queer Chick: A Guide to Sex, Love, and Life for Girls who Dig Girls *(Plume, 2016).* *Her fiction has appeared in* The Fiends in the Furrows *(Nosetouch, 2018),* Tiny Nightmares *(Catapult, 2020),* Grimdark Magazine, *and numerous other publications. She lives in Denver, CO.*

FARM-TO-TABLE

Sonora Taylor

Everything about this date was terrible. The restaurant lost Heidi's reservation, meaning they had to wait an extra hour for their table. That extra hour was spent with a man named Tate who looked as good as his profile picture, but was otherwise insufferable. His favorite topic was himself, and his favorite hobby was interrupting. Heidi sipped her wine, then puckered her lips. And now, the wine they'd been served tasted like someone had served them the vinaigrette by mistake.

Heidi sighed as Tate droned on and on about himself. She took a bite of her salad. Bland and tasteless. Of course. She considered pouring her glass of wine on it to add some flavor.

An unexpected crunch disrupted her chewing. Heidi scrunched her face. She'd only ordered simple greens with dressing. If anything was getting crunched in that bite, it was a piece of dirt. Heidi took another bite and felt another grainy crunch, which confirmed her suspicions. She hated when she accidentally ate granules of dirt left behind in vegetables. Maybe everyone else was big on farm-to-table dining, but she didn't need this blatant of a reminder of where her food came from.

"Everything okay with the salad?" Tate asked.

"Kinda tasteless," Heidi said. "Except for some dirt in the—"

"Maybe the dirt'll add some flavor." Tate grinned, and Heidi saw a black sesame seed in his teeth from his gyoza.

"Right." Heidi knew that anything more than two words would just be interrupted. Tate continued talking about his job, while Heidi tried to mentally count the minutes until she could politely leave and get the hell home—preferably with a pizza and her vibrator in hand within the hour.

She took another bite of salad, one thankfully devoid of dirt. The bite, however, seemed determined to stay above her throat. Its leaves brushed and tickled her throat as it slid down as slowly as possible. She reached for her wine, then thought better of it and reached for her water.

"So what do you do?" Tate asked.

"I—" Heidi stopped when her voice croaked around the lettuce. She held up her finger to ask him to wait, then took three big gulps of water. The bite of lettuce finally slid down her throat.

"You swallow salad?" Tate asked, with a dumb grin.

"No," Heidi said, before coughing once to clear her throat. The cough left behind an itchy sensation, as if the dirt granules she'd chewed earlier had planted themselves in her esophagus. "I write— *hmm hmm*—for a local blog—*hmm HMM*—I write restaurant reviews—*HMM!*" She cleared her throat and coughed again. The granular, itchy sensation wouldn't cease. It almost felt like it was spreading.

"You sick?" Tate asked, with genuine concern, though Heidi figured that concern was ninety-nine percent for himself.

"No, it's—" Heidi's eyes widened as she felt something tickle up onto her tongue. She pushed the object forward with her tongue, then pulled it out. It was a single leaf.

"It's the salad," she finished.

"Come on, that's gross," Tate said, with a sneer.

"This didn't come from the salad though," Heidi said as she held up the leaf. It was small and bright green, like a tender sprout in a spring garden.

"I still don't need to see food coming out of your mouth."

"Will you shut—" Heidi's throat burned and her mouth filled with leaves crawling over her tongue. She clamped her mouth shut, but kept coughing to try and ease the scratching sensation. The granules made their presence known in her throat, and Heidi felt as if they had tendrils growing from where they were lodged. Sharp, scratchy tendrils, almost like—

"Hailey, are you choking?" Tate asked.

"It's Heidi—" The leaves burst from her mouth, and the tendrils in her throat shot out from behind. Her eyes widened and she screamed a gargled cry around a cluster of roots that sped forward. They cracked through her plate and pulled her headfirst onto the table.

"Holy shit!" Tate yelled as he jumped up. Other diners looked over and began to scream. Heidi tried to lift her head, but it held fast. The wooden roots scratched all the way down her throat and into her stomach. She swore she felt them branching through her chest, her legs, her arms, and her—

Wood splintered through her nails. Heidi cried around the roots and felt tears fall down her cheeks. She felt tender sprouts form on her cheeks as her tears rained down upon them. Her hands bled and the blood swirled into the wood as it cracked through the table. She then felt the most horrid sensation yet: the roots crawling up through her head.

"What the fu—" Tate stopped and began to cough. He spit out the sesame seed that was stuck in his teeth onto the table. Heidi looked up and noticed it was still too late for him. The white flowers and green leaves of a sesame plant were sprouting all over his hands. As her skull began to crack to make way for a tree, she couldn't help but be relieved that at least Tate was also having a terrible date.

SONORA TAYLOR is the award-winning author of several books, including Little Paranoias: Stories, *and* Seeing Things. *Her work has been published by Kandisha Press, Camden Park Press, Sirens Call Publications, and others. She lives in Arlington, Virginia, with her husband and a rescue dog. Visit her online at sonorawrites.com.*

THE LAST BREATH OF SUMMER

Jameson Grey

The beach was full of summer tourists: bright young things sunbathing, Mums and Dads playing beach boules and other games with their kids, surfers hoping for the next big wave.

Deller gazed at the blue Atlantic. A lone surfer was trying to catch a ride on the tame waves. Part of him wanted to call the surfer in.

"Not your remit, Deller. Observe and report," Jacks, his boss, had told him. Indeed, the visor was fitted with a camera, microphone and earpiece to record his observations. "Nothing like a bit of first-hand qualitative data to supplement the tech," Jacks added.

"Will the suit do its job?" Deller queried.

"We believe so. Of course, there are no guarantees… but that's why you're being paid so handsomely."

"If I survive…"

The surfer *was* coming in, but, as Deller looked to the horizon beyond, he didn't think the rider was going to make it back to the beach in time. He willed the surfer to paddle a little faster.

"Whatya doin', mister?"

"Huh?" Deller said, startled out of his reverie.

A boy had ventured over to the rock pools and was standing, somewhat dutifully, behind the cordon Deller had set up earlier.

"Just some research, kid. You shouldn't be over here."

"I know, I *can* read, I *am* eight."

Deller fought an undertow of panic in his guts. "Just looking at the rock pools here."

"Can I help?"

"I'm afraid not, my boss even made me wear this protective suit." Deller hated lying to the boy, but he wanted him away. He didn't want to see what happened *that* close up.

"Why?"

"He doesn't want me contaminating anything."

"What's con-tam-in-aging?"

"Messing things up."

"Oh, can I watch then?"

"Best not."

A voice called out. "Danny, we're going, come on."

"That's my dad, I'd better go." Danny sounded disappointed. "OK, bye now." And with that he ran off.

"Bye." Deller watched the boy reach his parent, saw them have a brief conversation, noticed the father looking over at him. Dad seemed satisfied with Danny's answer, and they turned away, heading towards the café and the car park. Danny twisted and offered a wave. Deller reciprocated the gesture and watched as the boy ran off ahead of his dad. *Hope you make it, kid.*

Deller returned his attention to the sea, scanning for the surfer. He was still paddling in – but now he was being chased, not by waves but a rolling sea mist.

"That's my cue," Deller muttered to himself. He glanced over at the beach to check whether anyone was looking at him, but the nearest couple was sunbathing and, beyond that, families remained engrossed in their games. Others *had* noticed the mist rolling in and were pointing out to sea. It seemed the surfer was waving to them as they did so, and the onlookers waved back, but Deller didn't think he was larking.

Behind and above him on the cliffs, nests of gulls and kittywakes began to clamour. They know something's awry, Deller thought. The baleful toll of a foghorn sounded, and Deller wondered if someone was up at the old lighthouse or if it were automated these days. He hoped it was the latter.

The peal rang out only the once, but Deller took it as confirmation he should act and pulled the visor over his head, quickly fastening the clasps to the neck of his suit. He checked there were no gaps around the visor's seal before speaking again.

"OK, Jacks, it's coming—let's hope this suit of yours holds up, eh?"

"Message received, Deller. We have visual too, but as the mist rolls in, tell us what you see. Your eyes are much better than any camera, no matter what the techies tell us."

Panic did not set in immediately. A sea mist on a hot summer's day, whilst unusual, is not uncommon, and the first screams were not given the attention they merited.

"Perhaps they're thinking they're shrieks of delight?" Deller commented.

"I don't think so, somehow," Jacks replied.

"I've moved a little closer, but I'm going to hang back. It could be dangerous once people start to lose it. I've got the binoculars; I'm going to take a look." Deller raised them to his eyes and focussed on the far end of the beach, where those initial screams had come from. A man was running blindly away from the mist, clutching his face, blood seeping through his fingers. The man's arms were turning red too.

Somehow the man kept running, stumbling, tripping over a young couple who'd sat up from their sunbathing. He fell face first into the sand and started writhing. Although he was a few hundred yards away, Deller heard the man's agonised cries. One of the sunbathers looked on in horror, then she, too, screamed and tried to stand up.

Behind her, the mist rolled thickly over the beach, and suddenly she and her partner were gone, swallowed up in the fog. Shortly afterwards, the still-writhing man also disappeared.

The family playing their game of boules had stopped and were running for the beach café, perhaps hoping it would offer some sort of safety. They were still some distance from it when the dad, who'd been carrying one of his kids, fell; before he could get up, the mist enveloped them.

Others were fleeing too.

Deller swung the binoculars from left to right, scanning for Danny, the young boy he'd spoken to earlier. He and his dad we were tracking the sea wall at the back of the beach, trying to stay far away from the thick fog as it glided diagonally across the sand. They reached the stone steps that led up to the café as the mist rolled in front of them, and Deller was unable to confirm whether they'd made it in time.

"What's happening, Deller?"

"Chaos, panic, what do you think?"

"And the mist?"

"It's burning them—like it did on those islands in South-East Asia. Like it's some sort of acid mist. I'm going to walk into it now. People are far enough away from me—it should be safe."

"My word, you're cold, Deller."

"That's why you wanted me to do this, isn't it?"

Not waiting for a response, Deller set off. The mist had rolled over at least two-thirds of the beach now. Deller could see no-one. He lowered the binoculars—they were useless now.

"OK, it can't be more than 50 yards away now," he reported. "I'm going to be walking into it soon. Wish me luck."

"Roger that."

Deller stopped walking as the mist enveloped him. It was thick, like cotton wool hanging in the air—he could barely see his hand through the visor. The beach was dense with silence. No people, no birds, not even the sea.

Deller spoke to break the eeriness: "It looks as though the suit's holding up. I can't see shit, but I'm going to try to keep walking." He paused. "You can see something through the camera lens, right? Was it this bad in Mindanao?"

"No Deller, I don't think so. And we can see, alright."

Although there was no bearing point from which to judge, Deller thought he'd walked far enough along the beach to be near the man he'd seen perish first. He slowed, looking down at the same time. Even at a snail's pace, the lack of visibility was such that he tripped over the body when he found it. Well, what was left of it.

Deller forced himself to crouch beside the remains. "Are you seeing this?"

"We are."

"It's like it's melted his flesh and muscle clean away. Even his bone looks worn. Jesus, what is this stuff?" Deller turned to his right and saw the young couple, similarly wasted away. They'd been holding hands when they perished.

"I tell you what, I'm glad I'm wearing this suit."

"I bet you are, Deller. Our met pictures are showing that the mist is just about over you now. Is it starting to clear?"

Deller stood up. It did indeed look like it was thinning out a little. "Affirmative. I think I'm starting to see through it. Is it dissipating rapidly inland?"

"We're monitoring that—will come back to you shortly."

The mist continued to clear as it drifted inland, but as Deller surveyed the beach, he wished it wouldn't. All around were bodies burned away to bone and rag. He saw the corpses—one big, one small—of the dad who'd been holding his daughter. Even in skeletal form, they appeared to be clinging to each together. It reminded Deller of the petrified remains at Pompeii—loved ones eternally captured in their final, terrible, embraces.

He walked over to the stone steps that led off the beach and up to the café. Had Danny and his dad reached safety? At the top of the steps, the worst was confirmed: another pair of corpses—one big, one small.

"Geez, Jacks, seriously, what is it? Did some new chemical weapon leak?" There was no response. "Jacks?"

"Apologies, Deller, we're a little distracted here. The mist's not dissipating; it's continuing to roll inland, heading our way, in fact." Jacks sounded more distant than the five miles Deller knew him to be. "But... to answer your question, no we don't think it's a leaked weapon, at least not one anyone is owning up to. Even if it were, would it really travel like this?"

"No, I guess not, but something needs to be done. Summer's almost over, mist and fog's going to get a lot more prevalent come autumn."

Deller considered for a moment. "Are people being warned of the immediate danger? You won't be able to hush this one up."

There was a slight pause before Jacks responded: "We're more concerned about preserving ourselves at the moment." Deller heard furious activity from what he knew to be the back of the surveillance van. "We're going offline for a little while. We're going to try to drive away from it."

"What should I do?"

"My advice, old friend… keep your suit on."

Deller thought he heard a screech of tyres, a thud, what sounded like the beginning of a scream, then radio silence.

"Jacks?" No answer. "Jacks, are you there? JACKS!"

That silence didn't sound good.

Deller sat on the top step, lost in thought. Perhaps the mist augured doom? Was whatever caused it the hubristic mistake that marked the beginning of the end? He smiled bitterly. Perhaps the planet had had enough of our toxic behaviour, and this is its way of saying, "That's it, thank you, bye-bye!"

He tried one last time to raise Jacks on the radio.

Still no response.

"If you're listening, Jacks, there's time for one more observation."

Taking a final look at the scene of devastation on the beach, Deller slowly began to unclasp the clips on his visor, readying himself for the last breath of summer.

JAMESON GREY is originally from England but now lives with his family in western Canada. His work has been published by Ghost Orchid Press, Black Hare Press and Hellbound Books as well as in Trembling with Fear, Dark Dispatch *and* The Birdseed. *He can be found at jameson-grey.com and occasionally on Twitter @thejamesongrey.*

TURNING THE EARTH

Samuel Best

Dad was on nightshifts that week so we had to keep the noise down, otherwise he would wake up in a mood. He was usually in a mood, but when we woke him up it was always worse. He would slurp his tea harshly. He would shut the cutlery drawer and let it make that hard, sharp slap against the unit. He would brood until the whole house was filled with a thick, syrupy atmosphere that made me want to scrub my skin raw or move into that old shed in the middle of the woods.

I was in the garden, helping Mum with the plants. Like all children, I had chores to do. One of them was making Dad a cup of tea and leaving it by his bed for when he woke up. One of them was scrubbing the pots until they were clean and shiny. One of them was always being as quiet as a mouse. One of them was helping Mum sort the garden out.

Today, Mum was moving plants from little pots to big pots, their leaves waving in the breeze and tickling my skin. Sometimes she would stop and tell me about a plant, about whether it was good to use in cooking, or if it had a long scientific name, or about if it had poisonous leaves or sap or berries. Those were the ones Mum said I wasn't allowed to help her with, even if I really wanted to.

We had been in the garden for a while and my hands were brown and smelled strange, and Mum had a smear of soil on her cheek. We had done five pots so far and still had another five to go. We weren't talking much, but it was still nice being outside with her. The sun was bright and hot, and I don't think either of us thought much about Dad the whole time we were out there.

Until I dropped the pot. It happened so fast I barely saw it, but the sound seemed to happen in slow motion. It lingered on the hot air, echoing around the garden and up up up right into his bedroom. I tried to scramble the pieces back together, as if by fixing the pot we might cancel out the noise somehow, but there was a piece I couldn't find, and Mum told me to stop in case I hurt myself. She was standing up by then, facing the house like a soldier at inspection.

But the house was still. We waited for an age before I looked at Mum. She was moving her eyes between the back door and Dad's bedroom window, but there was no movement, no sign of anything. My pulse quickened and I thought that maybe we had gotten away with it. Mum looked at me then, but instead of looking happy or excited she still looked worried. I didn't understand it. She told me to wait there and went inside.

I waited for a little while, but my curiosity was too much in the end. I went inside too, and walked through the house like a phantom; soundless, not touching anything, jumping the stair that creaked. Upstairs, I could hear a quiet sound that made me stop and listen for a while. I followed it to Dad's bedroom and stopped at the door. It was louder in there, and I knew it was Mum. Very slowly, I pushed the door open. The door used to creak, so I had to be careful, but I managed to do it without making a sound.

In the bedroom, I saw Mum. She was next to Dad's bed, crouching down like she was praying. She wasn't speaking, though. She was crying. The noise came from her like it was catching in her throat. Small and choked. I moved forwards and saw Dad.

He was lying in bed like normal. Except this wasn't normal. One of his hands was out of the duvet and Mum was holding it but it looked strange, like it wasn't a real hand. Like it was a wax hand. Pale. Cold. Mum didn't notice me, I don't think, until I went even closer. I stood over her and put my hand on her shoulder. Her body was shaking as she cried and I took a deep breath as I moved my eyes from the back of her head to Dad's face.

Except my eyes didn't make it as far as Dad's face. Instead, they stopped on his cup of tea. It was still on his bedside table where I'd left it, except half the tea was gone. I looked back at Mum to see if she had noticed anything, but she was still crying. I moved around her and took the cup away. In the bathroom I poured the tea into the toilet and flushed, watching the brown water swirl away, taking with it those special, forbidden leaves from the garden, and my Dad. I realised then that Mum really did know her stuff when it came to plants. I rinsed the cup and went back through.

SAMUEL BEST is a teacher and writer from Scotland. His début novel Shop Front *was described as "a howl and a sigh from Generation Austerity", and he founded the literary magazines* Octavius *and* Aloe. *His short fiction has been published in magazines in Britain, North America, and Scandinavia. You can find him on social media* @storiesbysamuel.

LOCUST

Allison Floyd

This morning
she found a locust
outside her front door.
She'd had a lifetime of that,
always the sense of things
vague, green,
fluttering, forbidden
flitting on the periphery.
When she was young
she couldn't let herself
have things. The wine
soured on her lips.
It made her retch,
threatened to set things free
that she kept captive
in plastic containers,
and she would use

blank sheets of paper

to slide neatly beneath

the writhing bodies

once she had placed

the transparent domes

over them

so she could turn

their prisons

right side up

and seal the lids.

ALLISON FLOYD's work has appeared on Defenestrationism.net, the Submittable blog, On Spec Magazine, *and in the* Dark Hearts *anthology by Ghost Orchid Press.*

IMMORTALITY EXPIRED

Micah Castle

Life happens, things happen; we all just happened to be there when an asteroid crashed into Europe. Deep enough that no one knew if any *real* damage had been done. Obviously it *had*, but was it worth the time, money, and effort to learn anything more besides that there was a seemingly bottomless hole in the planet?

I'm sorry I'm rambling, but let me finish.

Wait—don't leave. I haven't spoken to anyone else in ages.

Thanks.

Yes, you can have more of my water.

The governments couldn't come to an agreement, so they did nothing but shield it from the masses. Every news channel showed the massive hole protected by police barriers and men in blue. Hordes of people surrounded them, holding up cameras and cell phones. Viewers only saw the absolute darkness within the miles-long rim. It was like God poked a little *too* hard.

We learned the governments were too slow on the take, because the Earth quickly changed how the ecosystem and humanity functioned. For better and worse.

It gave *more* life, *more* sentience; blew a miracle into the world's fibers, and it passed along to us.

I know you know what happened.

We're living it, but let me tell the story, please?

It's been so long that I almost forgot how to talk.

You can do that, you know?

OK, I'll hurry up.

At the beginning, we could still die naturally: old age, disease, et cetera. Then, there were a high number of reports of failing suicides. People tried jumping off bridges, attempted to shoot or hang themselves, overdose; you name it, they did it... But none worked.

Interviews flooded every media outlet with details about how when the jumpers jumped, vines saved them; when the shooters pulled the trigger, there weren't bullets but daisies; when pill-poppers downed a handful of meds it only calmed their bellies.

It took an army of scientists to figure out that the Earth—the asteroid—saved them. The planet would no longer allow suicide, and would keep us alive.

It was great, initially. People cheered in the streets; bars gave out free drinks; restaurants did two-for-one specials; and corporations celebrated with commercials and special-flavored items. It felt like we were all having one enormous, international party, like we weren't divided; like there wasn't a billionaire who saw dollar signs and hired bioengineers to alter the genes the asteroid mutated, and created a cure-all serum.

I know I sound like an asshole.

But look around us: was he right?

Were *we* right?

Animals once frolicked over there in the grass.

Now look; nothing but sand.

We have this smidge of bottled water.

We're not meant to live forever.

The Earth knew that, but we didn't.

Sort of like God.

Oh, you believe in Him?

Sorry.

Don't leave.

Have a drink, it's no problem.

Society was ecstatic.

We finally had a cure for the incurable diseases, as well as dying. Many religions rewrote their books and tenets about the End of the World to make more sense, now that we couldn't pass on. Even gas prices and taxes went down, too.

But we kept raping the land and killing animals en masse; decimating the sea and what dwindling life lived below. Dumping trash anywhere possible; vomiting toxicity into the sky, ignoring the expanding tear in the atmosphere.

Winters became summers.

Summers became blistering.

Years trudged along. So many babies made; so many mouths to feed and shit to clean, and no one died, and I was surprised that people were surprised when the global death count up-ticked.

We were at overcapacity before, but now... The cord snapped, the floor gave out; the planet told us we were over the weight limit for this ride, and could we stand aside to let the smarter species on?

Where are you going?

Come back, sit.

Have some more water.

It's getting dark, and it's dangerous at nightfall.

You're safer here.

You can't see them, but there's Jumpers.

You don't know what a Jumper is?

Folks took to living underground when everything went to hell. They couldn't stand the heat, and believed that if they lived underground, the Earth would keep them alive.

How?

No idea. Maybe provide nourishment through roots or something.

What do they do?

They sleep during the day, but at night they're awake. When something comes by, they jump out, and drag them into their cubbies. Kill and eat them.

People gotta survive, and Jumpers don't care what it is. Honestly, we shouldn't be picky either, but I'm not eating any human. Probably tastes horrible.

How do they live without water?

That's better left unanswered.

Like I said, the planet was tired of our bullshit. It couldn't save everyone. The cure was still shipped to every corner of the world, and the money kept rolling in for the lucky few.

Then the wealthy started dying, then the scientists, researchers, all the geniuses who gave us immortality… Factories still churned out the cure, and med centers dosed anyone willing to roll up their sleeve.

We still believed we could make it through.

We were so stupid. Putting faith in the idea that we would live forever peacefully. Who could've guessed immortality had an expiration date?

The cure stopped working.

In our bodies, in the foundries, everywhere.

Everything spawned from the first batch went sour. People who should've died years ago dropped like flies. People our age were only more tired than usual. But all the big players in the world were gone.

Every hour a new death was announced: billionaires, politicians, CEOs, CFOs, etc.

No one worth a damn remained. Without a leader, the underlings wouldn't tamper with the planet's genes. Terrified that they, too, would screw up as much as their bosses did.

So their focus turned from society to *themselves*.

Easier to save one than a million, right?

They shot for the Moon, literally.

Space stations and rocket ships and space travel became the new thing. Despite none of us having the luxury to go space-side, it was still crammed down our throats from everywhere imaginable. Big advancements in space technologies and planet colonization were made, and soon those holding all the chips were *gone*.

Game over.

No big money, no cure; a dying world.

And people *still* procreated.

We learned *nothing*.

Oh?

You had a baby during that time?

Where are they now?

Oh…

Sorry for your loss.

Me? No, never. Not one for children.

Had Lucy, a cat, though. Ran off—

I know it's not like having a kid.

Still miss her…

Sure, you can have the rest of the water.

Where was I…

Too many mouths to feed and not enough room to bury the dead.

Paints a pretty bleak picture, huh?

The former became the latter soon and, no matter the family's pleas, were cremated.

I can still smell and taste them, that sour, rotten air.

All the while, the Earth became impatient, and wanted us to hurry up.

Mother Nature's a fickle bitch.

An airborne disease blew in from God knows where. Got through our orifices and devoured us from the inside out. No big money, so no cure.

Thousands of people died. Crematories and funeral homes were jam-packed, even those who re-opened after shutting down during the Immortal Era. We quickly learned, after weeks of dumping, that the hole the asteroid created wasn't bottomless after all.

We sent some into space, but that ended up costing too much.

No, I don't have any lights.

They bring unwanted attention.

Not just Jumpers out there, you know.

Leerers and Lurkers, Stalkers and Eaters.

That's why I stay in this cellar. Shadows keep me hidden, the cement keeps me cool, and the collapsed wall lets me keep an eye out.

Nah, go ahead, finish it off.

I'll collect more tomorrow.

Not much else to say… We kept dying but couldn't kill ourselves.

We were imprisoned in a planet-sized cell.

Soon there were more bodies than babies.

Buildings fell to ruin, and nature gave up. Corpses became hills that baked in the sun. No food left. Disease mutated, and what's out there is a distant relative to the one that began everything.

I wonder if this was the Earth's plan all along. Give us a death sentence in the guise of a miracle. Or did it happen naturally, not caring of the consequences? Like earthquakes, tsunamis… We just happened to be at the wrong place at the wrong time.

Some could say an asteroid isn't natural, but where are they now?

Getting sleepy?

That happens.

The stuff I put in the water does that.

Took longer than usual, but I guess that's why they call me a Waiter.

What was in there?

Does it matter?

Just relax.

Good.

Limbs feel heavy?

Heartbeat sluggish?

All normal.

Don't fight it.

No more pain after this.

Let it take you.

Sooner you sleep, sooner this'll be over.

MICAH CASTLE is a weird fiction and horror writer. His stories have appeared in various magazines, websites, and anthologies, and has three collections currently out.

While away from the keyboard, he enjoys spending time with his wife, spending hours hiking through the woods, playing with his animals, and can typically be found reading a book somewhere in his Pennsylvania home.

You can find him on Twitter @micah_castle, Reddit r/MicahCastle, and on micahcastle.com.

THE UYTOROI

Zé Burns

Old Man Harris paid Benny a dollar for every golf ball he found on the beach. The aging restaurateur hit them out into Puget Sound from his waterfront tee. At low tide, the young man—a sack over his shoulder—would hunt for them. Benny came across many treasures on the beach: frosted glass, agates, moon snail shells, sea stars, anemones, little gelatinous puddles that were once jellyfish— memories from his childhood.

Benny knew to sidestep the holes in the sand where clams expelled streams of water, knew to hold his breath whenever he saw the orange carapace of a dead crab, and could judge just how far he could go out on a sandbar without being trapped by the tide. The briny air was nectar to him; the lap of the waves, music. In short, Benny couldn't think of anywhere he would rather be—the twenty-some bucks he made in a day were the icing on the cake.

That afternoon was the lowest tide of the year. Benny studied the charts religiously; they were his sacred texts. He'd been anticipating this day for months now. Not only would it prove lucrative—he could fetch golf balls that he couldn't normally reach—but he would find so many more treasures.

With his gumboots slurping through the mud, he thought of the fat purple sea stars that only appeared at the lowest tides. He hopped a rivulet and then another, a pip in his step. A yellowing golf ball stuck out near a barnacled rock, the word TITLEIST all but worn off. He picked it up, wiped off the kelp on his shirtsleeve, and tossed it in the sack.

Benny was almost to the waterline when he noticed a new addition to the menagerie of sea life. A milky white blob peered out of the sand. The shape and size of a soda can, its thick, soft skin seemed to absorb the sunlight. Could it be the polyp of an anemone? As he approached, he noticed it pulsating.

"Hey, little fella. I've never seen you before." Benny leaned in for a closer look and was greeted with a whiff of ammonia. He jerked back, his sinuses burning, and noticed the polyp turn toward him. Benny took a step to the left, then a step to the right. It moved with him.

"You're quite the find, my stinky friend." He played the back-and-forth game with it for a few minutes before continuing on his ball hunt. Benny shuffled through the next day. Sleep had evaded him with nightmare after nightmare. Around four a.m., he had given up and spent the morning drinking dishwater-flavored coffee in his van.

He sauntered along the beach, less interested in the sea life, when he saw the polyp. It was in a different location, a hundred yards away.

Forgetting the golf balls, he approached, with more caution this time. It stood a couple inches taller than the one from the day before. Three baby nodes congregated around its base. As before, it followed his movements. He pinched his nose and bent toward it.

"You have yourself a little family, eh?"

On the top of the polyp, a milky sphere opened up, almost like … an eye. It blinked once at him.

"What *are* you?"

Uytoroi.

Benny jerked up. Where had that come from? The word reverberated in his head. He looked down at the polyp once more. It winked its eye.

After another night of twisted things haunting his dreams, Benny spent the morning scouring the local library, going through book after book on Northwest sea life. He could find no picture resembling the malodorous polyps. Likewise, he couldn't find the word "Uytoroi" on the web, despite a dozen different spellings.

When he returned to the beach that day, Benny discovered a dozen polyps littering the beach outside Old Man Harris's house. But it was not the number that surprised him as much the *size*. The polyps stood a full foot tall, eight inches in diameter. When he went to fetch the sack from Harris's shed, he saw the old man approach. Their interactions were limited, a few words once a week at most.

"Hello, Mr. Harris."

"You've seen them too?"

"Hm? Oh, the polyps, yes."

"Nasty-smelling things, aren't they?"

"They *are* pungent."

"Listen," said Harris, leaning in as if someone could overhear him. "How would you like to make a few extra bucks?"

"Yes, definitely." Benny would've loved to eat something other than instant ramen for dinner.

"I'll pay you ten bucks a head to get rid of those nasty buggers. Just be discreet. We don't want the county involved."

A hundred and twenty dollars sounded mighty pleasant. "Sure."

The old man grunted. "Well, get to it." He went back into the house.

Benny respected the life on the beach, careful not to bother a single rock that might house a family of crabs. Maybe he could relocate the polyps, find them a new home.

He fetched a shovel from the shed and made his way onto the beach. The polyps turned to him all at once, a dozen opalescent eyes winking at him. "Don't worry, fellas. I won't hurt you. Just a change of scenery."

Benny plunged the spade into the muddy sand a foot away from the closest polyp. Hopefully, he could dig around the creature without damaging it. The white eye watched him, riveted.

He'd seen geoduck hunters dig holes three feet deep to extricate the giant clams. While the polyp was rooted beneath the sand, he couldn't imagine it would go that deep. But as he shoveled away, water filling the hole as he went, he discovered how deep down the polyp truly was. The alabaster node was just the top of the creature. Its true form extended over a yard into the ground and Benny still hadn't found the root. Meanwhile, the hot August sun beat down on him, his exertion glistening his skin. Over an hour later, he hadn't extracted the first polyp.

He wanted that money. *Bad.* But was it worth this poor creature's life? Especially a creature that seemed so intelligent, so curious?

Benny rounded the hole to stand over the polyp, his shovel ready to slice into it, when the words returned.

Why are you killing us? The voice was genderless, more of a static whisper than an actual voice. Benny looked around, though he was certain it came from the creature.

"I ... I ..."

Why do you hate us?

"I don't."

That weapon says differently.

"It's just a shovel."

That you mean to kill us with.

"I'm sorry. The man who lives here, he asked me to move you."

We see. Come closer.

Benny held his breath and leaned into the polyp. A plume of moisture shot from its eye, blinding him. He fell into a paroxysm of coughing. The world spun around him until he fell flat on his face, fading... fading. With his last conscious breath, he inhaled the ocean's perfume and all went black.

"Are you all right?" Old Man Harris prodded Benny's prone form. "Hey, Benny, Benny, wake up."

The younger man's eyes snapped open and the old man retreated. "Your eyes ... they're *yellow*. Are you all right?"

"I am all right," said Benny, rising to his feet with surprising ease.

"Did you pass out?"

"I passed out."

"Come inside. I'll get you something strong to drink." Harris hefted the shovel and led Benny across the beach. The eyes of every polyp followed them. Up the stairs, they reached a patio. "Sit here. Scotch all right?"

"Scotch all right."

Benny stared blankly at the brick wall of the house, his face a waxen mask, while the man busied himself inside. When Harris emerged, the young man was standing once more, the shovel in his hands.

"What's going on?"

Benny brought the shovel down on the old man's head, knocking him to the ground. Harris groaned, writhing on the deck, blood dripping down his temples. He struggled to rise, but fell flat on his belly. "*Why?*"

"We are the Uytoroi." The words came from Benny's lips, but it was not his voice.

"What?"

"We are the Uytoroi!" the voice screamed. "And we will do unto you what you would have done to us." Raising the shovel above his head, what was once Benny plunged it down into the man's neck, fracturing his spine. After a half dozen more blows, the neck was severed, blood pooling on the deck. Benny reached down, grabbed the head by its hair, and tossed it to the closest polyp. The creature extended its neck and coiled around it, gorging itself as it sucked the flesh from the bone.

Benny turned to the Uytoroi as they focused on him. "What do you ask of me, my masters?"

You have whetted our appetite. Now we are hungry.

ZÉ BURNS writes fiction, both horrific and bizarre. He is the editor-in-chief of the online surrealist arts magazine Babou 691. *His work has previously appeared on* Bizarro Central. *He lives in Seattle with his cat and a mountain of books that threatens to crush him in his sleep. You can find him at zeburns.com or on Twitter @ZeBurns.*

YOU CAN'T HAVE AN ORCHARD WITHOUT FRUIT

Corey Farrenkopf

The roots clung to soil, but the branches dropped their leaves, bark molting to a crisp. The sun felt like an ever-present eye on the horizon. Rays of heat wavered in the air, undulating like thin bodies throughout the orchard, shimmering ghosts of harvests past.

The pears were blighted. The peaches and nectarines were devoured by some insect native to the other side of the world, mandibles working over sweet flesh, only cores and rind left to stem. Eventually, there was nothing left for Sven to graft, no fresh cuttings to ensure the survival of an heirloom lineage of apple stretching back to the 1700s. The variety had been in the family since before they emigrated, before the house and the barn and the silos crept from the dirt, raised aloft by the buried hands of the dead.

Sven's children asked where the leaves had gone, why the branches bent back, bark splitting, exposing soft cambia beneath.

"That's a long list," he replied.

"Will they ever come back?" his children asked.

"With time, maybe."

But time did not bring back growth. Rain refused to weep from the sky. Blight had been absolute. Those wavering spirits, the mirage-thin bodies of heat, blackened and curled each new leaf.

You can't have an orchard without trees, without fruit, Sven whispered to himself each night, the whole family clustered in a single air-conditioned room while the rest of the house sweat through the night.

"Just sleep," his wife, Leigh, would say. But sleep only brought dreams of the darkest hue, endless rows of trees bending to the soil, shedding their skin, exposing something darker within. He could feel the generations behind him staring out through the rends in the bark, accusing, judging his failure to goad one more flush from their fields.

The children grew thin, skulls coming to the surface. Leigh suffered the same inward warp, joints all bone, skin nearly translucent over neck and wrist, clothes hanging off her frame like a poorly stuffed scarecrow.

"How much more time?" the children asked.

"I wish I knew. No one has that calendar," Sven replied, eyes tracing a wavering shadow of heat as it crept towards the family burial plot, the graying stones moss-spotted, some broken at the base, reclining back into the burnt grass and weeds that choked the plot.

Apples never grew true from seed. They required grafting, a branch from an established cultivar bound to hearty root stock, taped until the bond settled. Sven had nothing left to graft, no healthy tree to offer up a limb. With his children growing thin, stomachs echoing in the night, Sven always found his eyes wandering to the cemetery. All those generations who managed to feed their young without issue. Sven knew those were different times, but nonetheless, the thought was there, never failing to whisper in his ear.

In the morning, Sven unearthed the shovels from the barn, handed them out to his children, and instructed them where to dig.

"Six feet down. Don't worry about the width," he said.

His children struggled under the weight of the soil, even though it was dry and blew away on the wind. Sweat creased their little faces, staining the threadbare shirts that clung to their backs. The headstones perched above looked down into the second graves, the deep trenches wrought from the land. When Sven's oldest struck a casket, he made everyone pause.

"Give me a few minutes," he said, pointing the children toward the stone wall wrapping the property.

When they were a distance off, Sven cracked open the casket of a long-buried uncle with the tip of his shovel. The wood splintered easily. Nothing but stained bones rested within, their garments moldered away. Teeth ringed the skull like a necklace.

Sven gathered the bones, erecting a neat pile by the grave's edge. When all were removed, he called his children back, tasking them with more digging, but making sure they knew to stop when they struck wood. He didn't want any of them following him through the next step.

While the children dug, Sven gathered the bones in his arms and walked down to the orchard, his grafting tools already at the base of an old Cherry tree.

It took time, but Sven managed the necessary cuts, the new joints, pale bone arching out where burnt branch once bent. The trees looked garlanded with femurs and ulnas, ribs draping down towards the ground. He did his best to keep the hands intact, palms out, fingers reaching towards the sky.

Sven exhumed the countless dead of his family, dropping into the holes his children dug, unearthing what lay inside. He worked himself to exhaustion, always giving his children what little water they had, rather than hydrating himself. Over the course of a week, he transformed a half-acre into an orchard of bone, skeletal hands pointing towards the barren sky, pleading with whatever god was out there to deposit something edible in their palms.

"We'll sleep beneath the trees," Sven told his wife and children. "There's a nice breeze tonight. Maybe the time is now."

No one argued.

The whole family unfurled sheets over the browned grass, newly erected branches overhead. Wind rattled the grafts like cryptic wind chimes, hollowly clocking in time to each gust.

In the morning, the children woke to the creaking of the palms, skeletal hands bending down towards them, grasping ripe pomegranates and apples, peaches and plums. The hands released their fruit when the childrens' fingers twined with their own.

The children ate greedily, empty stomachs desperate for the soft, sweet flesh.

As they ate, Leigh moved to Sven's side, nudging him, trying to call him from slumber. But he wouldn't rise. In his pocket, she pulled out a note written in his quick hand, only legible from years of familiarity.

If the time is now, bury me with the rest. Tell the children to wait. Soon I will be ready to grow anew.

Leigh creased the note, tucking it into the folds of her dress, before she began to drag her husband's body towards the family plot, not wanting to disturb her children from their harvest.

COREY FARRENKOPF lives on Cape Cod with his wife, Gabrielle, and works as a librarian. He is the fiction editor for The Cape Cod Poetry Review. *His work has been published in* The Southwest Review, Catapult, Tiny Nightmares, Reckoning, Flash Fiction Online, Bourbon Penn, *and elsewhere. To learn more, follow him on twitter* @CoreyFarrenkopf *or on the web at CoreyFarrenkopf.com*

AEQUINOCTIUM

Marisca Pichette

behind my lungs she whispers
too deep.

In her echo my toes seek mycelium & darkness
holes widen to hold me
but moss recoils, knows
I am a stranger.

I promised to stop but I fight
ripping new wounds while my fractals form
underneath
she whispers
breathe once.

I gasp & gasp gasp gasp
clawing grass grasping
soil & rocks

hearing only her voice

my skin sprouts,

hardens where she planted me.

blink once.

Bark creeps across my eyes

stifles my voice while hers grows

a whisper to a gale.

Ax & spade are last to vanish,

consumed under my shroud

of withered leaves.

MARISCA PICHETTE is an author of speculative fiction, nonfiction, and poetry. Her work has appeared in PseudoPod, Daily Science Fiction, Apparition Lit, Mermaids Monthly *and* The NoSleep Podcast, *among others. Her debut novel,* Broken, *is forthcoming in August 2022 with Heroic Books. A lover of moss and monsters, she lives in Western Massachusetts. She is on Twitter as @MariscaPichette and Instagram as @marisca_write.*

SIXTY PERCENT

Jennifer Lee Rossman

Everything is water, and water is everything. It is the blood that pumps through every living thing, it is life and death, it is us.

Society rises and falls with water, at the capricious whims of the gods and nature, but let society rise too high, and it floods. Spilling across the land, drowning it, carving out ugly gouges with the accelerated erosion of industrialization and progress.

And then you have this, the drought of the century, if not the millennium, the ground cracking into dust and the few surviving plants dying of thirst before your eyes.

Your family's farm is one of uncountable thousands succumbing to the second dust bowl, just a drop in the fast-evaporating bucket. Your story of hardship and loss is no different from all the others vying for the bailouts you know won't be enough to do any good.

But this one is yours. Your family's, for three generations now.

You know better than to cry; it's a waste of hydration and you don't know when or where you'll get your next mouthful of clean water. But it's your farm, it's everything you've ever known. You can't stop your eyes from watering any more than you can stop that tear from rolling down your cheek and falling to the ground.

Now, if this were a different kind of story, a hopeful story, that one little tear would be the thing to save your farm. It would be full of magic and all the crops would spring back to life overnight and all your troubles would be over.

But this ain't that kind of story and hope is about as scarce as water these days. Oh, that one little tear is absolutely going to save your farm, just not in the way you want.

The next morning finds the earth even more thirsty and desperate. Part of you has given up on saving your crops, and worries about the species as a whole. If this keeps going on, will you starve or will the dehydration get you first? The way you're sweating in this heat, you're pretty sure it'll be the latter.

There's a buzzing at your ear; you swat it away but the bee comes back, hovering in front of your face. You can't remember the last time you saw a bee. Probably about the same time you last saw a flower.

It's staring at you.

Every time you wave your hand at it, the bee comes back, unbothered. Closer, closer. Looking you right in the eye.

You take a step back, nearly crushing the tiny green leaf that has sprouted where your tear fell yesterday. The bee follows. Another step, the bee gets even closer, until you can feel the wind from its wings on your eyelashes.

Flinging your hands up to protect your face, you take another step, but stumble, finding yourself flat on your back on the parched soil as the bee tries to crawl between your fingers.

More sweat prickles at your skin, from fear as much as the heat. The ground eagerly drinks it up, desperate for moisture, and the bee suddenly flies off.

You don't question what just happened; you just run inside.

More greenery has sprung up overnight. Little leaves, the beginnings of a vine. You can't see it from this perspective, but the new growth forms the perfect outline of your body from where you fell yesterday.

You know better than to call it a miracle, to let yourself believe your troubles are over. There's no such thing as miracles, just like there's no such thing as rain.

But it's your farm. It's your farm, and it's coming back to life, even now there's been no rain for what seems like years, and you just have to go out and take a closer look.

In your excitement, you don't notice the bees.

You don't notice any of the insects, or the little creatures drawn out of the dying woods by the promise of quenching their thirst. You certainly don't notice the vine that snaps up and curls around your ankle, not until you're face down in the dust and surrounded.

Water is everything, we are water. Sixty percent of our body, to be precise.

And nature knows that now.

JENNIFER LEE ROSSMAN (she/they) is a queer, disabled, and autistic author and editor from Binghamton, New York. They have been published in over 30 anthologies, two of which they co-edited.

Website: http://jenniferleerossman.blogspot.com
Twitter: @JenLRossman

FROM THE POLLINATORS, THE NEW WORLD ORDER

Clint White

She shouldn't be here, in this man's minivan, just before sunrise, next to an overgrown, unwanted property off the freeway, and she shouldn't be here because, though she was nearly legally divorced and could see whomever she pleased, this man was married, and she can still feel the acrid woozy pain that brought her to her knees the day she found her ex's texts, and especially the pictures, jesus christ the pictures, but now here she was, like the woman in those digital pictures, and yet, here was a man who kissed her differently, like she deserved admiration instead of an afterthought, and a thick fog hovered over the fields and lumbered towards the minivan, and all of this, it wasn't really about being wanted, it could just be curiosity, being the other woman for once, and as she rolled on top of him and pushed his shoulders against the backseat she felt powerful, like she was in control this time, and maybe his marriage was his problem to worry about, not hers, and she knew that wasn't exactly ethical, but everyone needs to feel powerful sometimes, and then he grabbed her chin and kissed her hard and raked his fingers across the scar tissue above her hip that made her tremble and shake and powerless when touched, and thoughts of ethics melted, and the varied anthers in the field around them spurted their pollens into the fog, and the fog carried them towards the lovers, and right when the fog perfectly enveloped the minivan, she perfectly enveloped him, and heard him gasp, and knew that he was the powerless one now, and what's power anyway except knowing someone needs only you, even if for just a moment, and as she rose and fell and the man beneath her whimpered, the fog crawled into the minivan and the heater core couldn't break the spores it carried from the ravenous weeds, and they both noticed a wild chill raking the backs of their necks and tumbling down their bare spines, particles of ecstasy, and they kept moving to silent music, fearing nothing but passion, like married lovers parked in steamed-up minivans everywhere, fucking their way through the rising action of their lives, fearing only the loss of passion, and despite the chill, they kept moving, and came closer to what they were seeking, and that's when she could feel her eyes burn and her throat burn and his marriage burn and her future burn and his voice caught and burned and they both burned and gave birth to new limb-laden things that the fog entrusted to their open ecstatic mouths and these new limb-laden things embraced each other in the steamy aftermath of their brief hosts, and just like them, they were so hungry.

*CLINT WHITE is an environmental lawyer and weird fiction author. His stories have appeared in anthologies from Ghost Orchid Press (*The Deep*), Black Hare Press (666), and Crow's Feet Journal (100 Ways to Die). He lives in Columbus, Ohio, with his librarian wife, two children, and a gentlemanly cat with very few teeth. Twitter @clintrwhite.*

FERTILIZER

Philine Schiller

Despite its appearance, the door doesn't creak. It swings open easily enough, rusty hinges and broken plastic glass giving way into a world of green and moisture. That's the thing you notice most, the wetness of it all. Water drips; it drips down the see-through ceiling and along the see-through walls, drips over gadgets and appliances and half-broken pipes, drips down leaves and vines. It feels like you dove under and into liquid steam. But the earth swallows it all, soaks it up and spits it back out like saliva, and the smell is not petrichor but deeper, more persistent.

The heat is oppressive, yet it feels lush and full. The air is like breathable food. You try to single out some of the scents as you step forward, a little lost and unsure where to turn, but they swirl like thoughts into your empty head and leave you feeling almost dizzy. Tomatoes?

Yes, you see them, out in the open room to your right, rows of them, splats of red between plants that rise high and stretch towards the ceiling. But what you smell are not the fruits. You touch the stems and sniff your fingers, and suddenly you're a child again, in a garden.

You can't quite place the memory; maybe it's many memories at once, maybe not even a real one, but the smell feels like home. You want to wrap yourself in it. And for a second you really believe you're there, wherever there is, you're there and there's someone staring at you in that garden. Someone you know? You try to see the face, but it's a blur. Then you're back in the greenhouse, but there's still someone staring at you. You turn around, and the feeling leaves you. There's no one there. Of course not.

They're held up by string, the plants, like hanged men. The tomatoes are ripe and plump. Some have ripped open, their tender flesh tearing apart the skin and spilling out onto the floor, seeds and juice and flesh, dripping sweet water into the earth. It makes you think of life and decay. You feel odd, but not in a bad way. The thick air fills your lungs. You can almost feel the strings around your throat, can almost feel like those hanged plants, can see yourself hanging amongst them.

If you breathe too much of this, you might drown. Small breaths now, shallow. Stay calm. It's just the heat.

But you are calm, you really are, despite the feeling that is expanding in your gut and all the way out into your fingertips. The image of you up on the wires, swinging there with rope around your neck, tomato juices coating your skin as the plants swallow you up, and then: your own skin ripping open, you spilling like the tomatoes...

it's there in your mind a little too vividly. You shudder. Why were you here again?

Right.

A favor. Your friend, asking you if you could water his plants. Maybe fertilize them, if you had the time. He couldn't make it, wasn't feeling well, but plants didn't take days off. They're always hungry, always demanding.

Take what you want, he said. *There's enough. And remember, the fertilizer needs to be worked into the earth. Don't just throw it on top.*

There really was enough. Curious, you walk towards the plants. The skin, when your fingers curl around the fruit, is smooth and firm. Skin on skin, you stand there, seizing each other up. Really, that's what it feels like, as if you're not just looking at the plant, but the plants are gazing back, all of them like one animal.

You're feeling odd again, almost embarrassed. It feels so intimate. Trying to shake your unease, you tug at the tomato. The panicle snaps, suddenly and easily. It's that scent again, fresh and sharp. And just like that, you're hungry.

You're so hungry. Starving, emaciated. There's a part of you that recoils from eating, something cautioning you, but you've always given into your hunger too easily. Stomach over guts. You bite into the tomato with a sort of violence, and you shudder as the delicate skin rips and your teeth tear through the sweet flesh. There's so much water, so much wetness, running down your throat and down your chin, and you feel as though you can finally breathe again, inside this damned, constricting, hot, green shack.

But with the eating comes the dread. No, not really—it's been there before, it was with you the whole time, but you'd pushed it back down. With the hunger quenched, there's nothing shielding you from reason. It's here now: The sudden, certain knowledge that you're an animal in a trap.

You're breathing heavily, the half-eaten tomato clenched in your hand, dripping like your mouth, the mush on your tongue suddenly feeling unpleasant, wrong. You can't bring yourself to swallow any more of it. You bend forward, let it spill from your lips, and watch the red liquid drip onto the wet earth, blood-like. This time, the feeling that someone is watching you does not go away.

Your friend, he'd told you once, that the shed beside the greenhouse was supposed to be haunted, and you'd both laughed. Maybe it's not haunted at all. Maybe the thing inside the greenhouse is another thing entirely. *Maybe he knew.* You don't know, and you don't much care to find out. You need to get out of here.

But where's the door? Where's anything? There are only plants, rows of plants, tight and tighter, high and narrow, blocking your way or luring you in deeper, you don't know. Deeper into what? *The belly of the beast*, you think. Your stomach revolts. You feel sick down to your bones. But you don't move, standing frozen, somehow knowing deep down that to move now would be death.

You understand the deer deep in the woods and the spider crowding into its dark corner, you understand that when you feel something hungry lock you in its gaze, you need to stay still. If you move, it will see you. If you run, it will hunt you. But you can't stay still forever. It will find you, then, too. Sooner or later, always death. You've never been so scared.

You take a step, just a small one. And then you're calm. It's a sudden calm, and you know you shouldn't be feeling it, you know it's bad, bad, but you're so very calm. Content. *It's got me*. But you don't care anymore. Maybe it's surrender, acceptance, or maybe it's like a poison inside of you, choking your reason with hand-like vines. It doesn't matter. You smile, open your mouth, taste tomatoes.

You're being fed, but you don't see by whom, you don't even see anything at all, though your eyes are open. You're somewhere else again—back in that garden? A child? Children need to be fed, before they can feed themselves, before they, in turn, feed others. Right. You understand that. You're being fed so you can feed others. That makes sense. It's not bad. It's alright.

You eat willingly. You eat until you're full, plump and ready to burst, and you lie down, crawling beneath the plants, curling around yourself. It's so hot. You lie there, not thinking anything at all. Sweat beads on your skin, mixing with the water dripping onto you from the leaves above. You look up, vision blurry. The ceiling is impossibly high. The sky behind it is disappearing. You feel like you're being hugged, and you smile as you see the vines and roots that are probing at your skin. You're not being hugged—you're being swallowed. No, buried.

Fertilizer needs to be buried. It needs to be worked into the earth. That's how they get the nutrients, that's how they turn out so sweet. Right. It's all good, right? You've done what you came here to do;

your job is done. You just need to rest now, rest a bit among the plants. You're tired, and you want to sleep, just for a moment.

It occurs to you that in the end you're not hanging up there on the wire at all, you're not like the taut, tied tomatoes, and the thought makes you laugh. No need to have been so worried. There's no string around your throat. Just the roots. The earth takes what it needs. It gives back bounty, beauty, plenty. But you're not the fruit. You're the fertilizer.

PHILINE SCHILLER is a doctoral student at the University of Heidelberg, Germany, where she received her M. Ed. for English and Spanish philology in 2020 and currently works in the department of education. Her academic and literary interests include contemporary literature, food studies, popular culture, fantasy, horror and science-fiction. Her twitter handle is @lines__lines.

a dryad arises

Jasmine Arch

roots grip dark damp earth
branches always reaching

swaying
to the touch of a breeze
leaning into the violence
of a storm

but nothing compares to the storm
that is man

i try to coax my trees to move
fight or flee
this blight that walks

but their slumber is too deep
their roots too strong

axe swinging
man stomps through
trampling sacred earth
uprooting fragile saplings

thwack thwack thwack
blade biting slender trunks

the eerie song of a two man saw
drowns out the melody of wind and bough

finally a tall oak rises

the treekiller's scream cut short
blood seeps into steadfast roots

these trees
are lambs no more
we are lions
we roar

JASMINE ARCH is a poet, writer, podcaster and narrator living in a little nook of Belgian countryside with two horses, entirely too many dogs, and a husband who knows better than to distract her when she's writing. Her work has appeared in NewMyths.com, Mermaids Monthly, *and* The Crypt, *among others. You can find her at JasmineArch.com or on Twitter @Jaye_Arch, or TikTok @jaztellsstories.*

TREEFINGERS

Hannah Hulbert

The low sun strobes through the trees as I drive along the avenue. Amber's turned the heating up, holding her hands near the air vents to thaw them out after our chilly walk. I flip down the visor and wish I'd brought my shades.

"I loved exploring here when I was little," Amber says, to fill the silence of my busted radio. "The beeches all have these twisted faces. I used to imagine they were a crazy extended family. Look! That one was the grumpy old uncle!"

I glance out the window and catch a glimpse of what she means. Gnarly knots have formed where branches have been lopped off and healed over, grotesque yet oddly endearing. Just the kind of thing Amber would notice. But I can't admire them while I'm driving, especially with the sun streaming between the trunks.

"They do resemble people," I say. "The branches are like arms arching across the road."

"Especially in the winter," Amber says. "I've always loved it here. Thanks for coming back with me." She pats my knee.

"No problem." I take her hand and give it a squeeze whilst keeping my other on the wheel.

It's only twenty minutes to her parent's house—the future in-laws. There'll be hot drinks and a fireside waiting for us; warm welcomes and tight hugs. I loosen the neck of my sweater, suddenly sweltering. I turn to Amber, but she's staring up at the bare limbs reaching above us, skeletal and dark against the fiery sunset. The scene is reflected in her eyes, which are wide with awe and wonder.

"It's like they're stretching out to stroke us," she says.

I focus on the road ahead again, but they're unavoidable: blackened bones dangling, surrounding us. It reminds me of a catacomb. Except these bodies are only half-buried and still alive, inching closer on every side, longing to embrace us...

I blink until I feel more alert, and turn down the heat.

"Hey, I'm cold!" Amber says.

"We'll be back soon. And I don't want to fall asleep before I get to that sofa."

"You're as bad as Dad," Amber laughs. "Resting your eyes!"

My lips form a thin line. Her parents' small living room is always stuffy and the ceaseless babble of antique and property programmes from their TV lulls me to sleep every time. I've made plans to be out as much as possible while we're visiting, but the season conspires against me and I don't want to seem unfriendly towards them. We are about to become legally bound, 'til death do us part, after all.

I force myself to take a long, deep breath.

"Don't they remind you of fingers?" Amber says.

"Sure," I say. But I'm imagining what kind of creature would have so many fingers, so long and skinny, with so many illogical joints. A shiver creeps up my sweaty spine.

"It's like they're one big tree, all joined together. Isn't it beautiful?"

Her voice is distant, as though it's echoing down a long tunnel of trunks to the left and the right, with spindly branches overhead and a web of roots below. My breathing's ragged and shallow: tiny, fearful gasps.

"What's the matter, Andrew?" she asks.

I shake my head rather than reply. My knuckles are white as I grasp the wheel. The sun's sinking behind a horizon hidden by the beech columns, darkening the patches of sky that flicker between the branches.

They're squeezing the road, tightening around us as we drive. I've never had a claustrophobia attack in a car before. What do I do?

"Why don't we pull over?" Amber suggests, putting her hand on top of mine.

The touch of her clammy skin is too much. I try to jerk my hand away, but it's clamped onto the wheel.

The car swerves across the road, careering towards one of the thick trunks. It grows larger and larger, filling the windscreen with its hideous lumpy face. Amber screams.

I haul on the wheel as we bump onto the verge, continue in a wide arc, then bounce back onto the tarmac. I straighten up and keep driving back the way we just came, heart hammering.

"Andrew, pull over," she says again, her voice shrill.

I can't. If I stay here they'll choke us both to death. I keep my foot down and the faint scent of burning rubber seeps inside.

"Andrew..." she says, but the arboreal tunnel consumes all my attention. It's closing in on us, claws straining to dig into the roof and tear it to shreds.

But then I realise, with a lurch in my gut, that the dangling twigs aren't fingers.

They're the tiny hairs on the backs of the knuckles.

Those faces are the arches, loops and whorls that make each tree unique.

The fingers aren't stooping to touch us. They're towering up from the soil on either side as we speed along the infinite life-line between.

Just below that glove of tarmac and soil, the mass of roots cups us. We barrel across the palm of the giant: infinitesimal specks powerless against its might. It sustains us and nurtures us and, on a whim, crushes us like bothersome bugs.

Above the growl of the engine and the pounding of my heartbeat, there's a small, damp sound. Amber's sobbing. I want to reach out and reassure her that it'll be okay, but I can't. I can't stop now while the hand of beeches is curling its hundreds of digits around us into a fist. The best thing I can do for her—for us—is escape.

The sunset's faded to an eerie twilight. I switch on my headlights and wish I hadn't. Shadows leap in every direction, looming over us and round us and under us in black bars. But I can just make out the empty sky at the end of the tunnel, a place where I'll be able to breathe again. I lock my eyes onto the pale horizon and lean on the steering wheel.

The car lurches. A bump in the road. I don't slow, but Amber cries out. I squint at the tarmac ahead. It's bulging and rippling with cracks. The sinews of the tree-hand pull taut as the thick digits draw into a fist. The headlights illuminate nothing but the wall of bark before us as we hurtle towards it. The sky has disappeared behind the stranglehold of the giant.

There's a smash and Amber and I jolt forward in our seats. A sharp pain crushes against my ribs, squashing the air from my lungs.

The metal shell around us groans and buckles as the trunks squeeze closer. They hold us still. Like a mother holds her anxious baby. Like a son holds the hand of his ageing father. Like a couple entwining their fingers. I reach for Amber.

The windscreen shatters, raining crystal confetti on us. Amber's silence is more alarming than any scream. I fumble with my safety belt, as if there might be something I can do to help her.

The beeches bow, wrapping themselves around the car. The metalwork screeches. The space inside is shrinking. I shake Amber, but she's still, her face so peaceful. I watch her sleep as the air is crushed from my body.

We didn't stand a chance. There were simply too many of them, already there, waiting for us. How can you escape something that's already there?

The trees cradle the wreckage of our vehicle, lifting us, cocooning us. The fingers caress the crumpled bodywork, groaning and scraping with those long, thin twigs. And then we collapse into the earth.

The last light of the sky disappears as the trees embrace us, binding us together. We are enfolded into the earth, tangled in that net of roots, welcomed into the family, forever.

HANNAH HULBERT is a full-time mum and part-time writer from the south coast of England. She enjoys looking for mushrooms, doings crafts, and drinking tea. Her stories have appeared in Metaphorosis, Lunar Station Quarterly *and the anthology* Cat Ladies of the Apocalypse, *among others.*

Website: https://hannahhulbert.wordpress.com
Twitter: https://twitter.com/hhulbert

INCIDENT IN KAYAPÓ

Isaac Menuza

Ministry of the Environment

DATE: 25 October 2022

SUBJECT: Incident in Kayapó

CONTENTS:

Transcript of voice memos belonging to Rafaela Murer, agent of the Brazilian Institute of the Environment and Renewable Natural Resources (IBAMA). Device recovered from investigation site (see attached map). Whereabouts of Agent Murer unknown.

Recording #1 — 3 September 2022; 23:14:36 AMT

AGENT MURER: Well, Maria, I didn't think it could happen, but things have gotten worse.

Our squad landed this morning deep in Kayapó Indigenous Territory north of the target garimpo. You wouldn't believe the sight of the land. Black landscape, trees burnt to matchsticks. Death *everywhere*. It made me want to vomit. Hélio [Comment: Agent Hélio Jobim] was furious. Spoiling for a fight. Can't blame him. I think we all hoped the miners would resist. Give us an excuse to crack their heads.

Six of us headed south on foot from the chopper. My balaclava stifled me; the flak vest weighed me down. Amazon heat is a living thing. João [Comment: Agent João Caldas] told me I could stay behind at the landing site with the pilot. He acts like *I'm* the rookie. The real problem is I don't have a penis. Not that his would be worth commenting upon.

We heard the hum of generators first, like mechanical insects. We checked our firearms, assembled in formation. The squad broke into a clearing of dirt and rust-colored puddles. We surrounded the tents that lined the lip of the crater. Water hoses snaked out of the hole like the Earth's intestines.

I took cover behind an earth mover, its engine running despite the fact we'd yet to see a living soul. Most likely the miners had been tipped off by our request for municipal access. How will we ever be able to do our job if the President insists we give the criminals a head start?

As I had feared, the settlement was empty. A ghost garimpo. Hélio cursed so loud a flock of birds took flight. Our squad explored all the way to the river. We found half-eaten food covered in flies, abandoned equipment, porn mags, handguns, false teeth, chainsaws, mud-caked boots, a pocket watch—everything but the idiotas themselves.

João thought he found a trail into the trees. Boot tracks. Fresh. He tried to convince Hélio we should follow. Gilberto [Comment: Agent Gilberto Fernandes]—the old timer I told you about—he and I argued we should raze the camp while it was unguarded. Can always count on Gilberto for common sense.

I had the pleasure of torching the earth mover. Threw a petrol-soaked rag into the cabin and watched the flames eat it. Beautiful.

When we'd finished, we confiscated the firearms and contraband, hauled it back to the chopper, all of us soaked in sweat.

We found our pilot's radio in the cockpit but the pilot himself was nowhere to be seen. We called for him. The trees swallowed it. I could tell from Gilberto's wrinkled scowl that he feared the worst. An ambush, maybe.

The squad argued. With nightfall approaching, we had zero chance of finding the pilot, though João flapped his arms and postured as if he might charge into the jungle himself. Hélio chewed his lip. Maybe he was considering it, but he decided to set out first thing in the morning instead.

We came back to the garimpo to spend the night. Good thing we left a few tents standing. I'm on watch now, in case the angry miners wander back. They could be waiting in the trees now…

Male voice, likely AGENT CALDAS: Rafaela. What are you doing?

MURER: Nothing. Just staying awake.

CALDAS: Be quiet. You want them to shoot you where you sit, fool girl?

MURER: Fuck you, João.

[Comment: Footsteps retreating]

MURER: I'm sorry, my love, that is all for now.

Recording #2 — 4 September 2022; 00:46:32 AMT

MURER: Maria, I dreamt you were alive. Maybe these recordings are a part of that dream. They fool me into thinking you're here with me, that I'm not utterly alone in this wilderness.

That there's still love in the world.

Recording #3 — 4 September 2022; 07:27:55 AMT

My God, Maria, you should have seen it. The most astounding bird I've ever encountered. Perhaps a Bellbird but brilliant red instead of white. Its breast was a mottled grey with black swirls like eyes or the knots in an ancient tree. Strong and regal, with a fleshy wattle like a sage's beard. It stared at me for a full minute. Grabbed my phone to snap a picture but must have startled it. Gone without a sound. I think—

Male voice, possibly AGENT JOBIM: Rafaela. Have you seen João?

MURER: Not since last night.

JOBIM: The idiota must have took off without us. Pack up. We have to go.

Recording #4 — 4 September 2022; 21:08:44 AMT

MURER: I can't. God. Gilberto…

[Comment: Sobbing until end of file.]

Recording #5 — 4 September 2022; 21:12:21 AMT

MURER: I think we're going to die out here.

Only Hélio and me now. He's trying to start the helicopter but the thing's been falling apart since the budget cuts. Wails like a wounded animal when he powers it. I don't think he knows how to fly it anyway…

God.

We found the pilot. João led us to him. Or his path did. A trail of bootprints and cast off equipment—gloves, socks, even his flak vest and camo trousers. Like he was carried off fully naked.

A little ways past João's discarded pants, the pilot's body sat against a huge trunk. His…

[Comment: Sobs.]

His hands were buried in his abdomen like… like he'd been digging for something… so much blood. Gilberto covered him with his jacket. I puked. Twice.

I don't know why, but the forest felt alive at that moment, almost joyful. As though I was a stage actor, and it the audience.

Hélio heard the sound first. A low rumble of white noise. He signaled for the rest of the squad to follow. There were five of us—Gilberto, Hélio, me, and the two rookies: Eduardo and Demian. They looked ready to bolt, eyes like jumbo eggs.

We broke through a wall of vines, stumbled into a torrent of fat flies. Deafening buzz of their million wings. They swarmed a heap of bodies. Our lost miners, judging by their ratty clothing and sun-shriveled skin. Strangest, though, the corpses had a... design. Arranged in a circle, and at the center, a single victim knelt, hands turned upward, eyes plucked from his skull.

Music. The sweetest song. Descending from the canopy. Filling my ears. I don't know if it was shock that made it so overwhelming, but we were all struck to stillness.

Then Gilberto, Demian, and Eduardo stumbled forward like drugged cattle. They stood in a triangle around the eyeless corpse, and each placed his gun in another's mouth.

I wanted to scream, but the music had clogged my throat.

João emerged from the brush on the other side of the men, chin and naked body smeared with gore, arms raised like a tattooed Jesus sleepwalking. His jaw ground side to side, and he spat a thick hunk of flesh into his hand. He smiled and held up his severed tongue.

Three gunshots exploded simultaneously, managing to briefly drown out the music and break our stupor. Gilberto and the other two men collapsed at the feet of a grinning João, heads turned to ragged craters. Hélio shoved me. Told me to run.

And I did. I'm such a coward. We didn't stop until we reached the helicopter.

Oh, Gilberto... What are we going to do now?

Unidentified voice, possibly AGENT CALDAS: [Unintelligible]

MURER: João? What the hell, man? What happened to you?

[Comment: Sound of a struggle. Device likely dropped.]

MURER: Get...off of me!

CALDAS: [Groaning] Can you...[Comment: Obscured. Requires further review.]...the eye?

MURER: [Choking sounds.]

JOBIM: João! Leave her alone!

[Comment: Sound of a struggle. Men grunting. Agent Murer coughing. Probable Agent Jobim screaming, then cut off abruptly.]

CALDAS: Mmmmmmmmmmm. Can...you...hear it?"

[Comment: Firearm discharged.]

MURER: Oh, João. What have you done?

Recording #6 — 5 September 2022; 01:08:31 AMT

[Comment: First seven minutes of recording wordless footsteps. Probable sound of Agent Murer walking in jungle environment.]

MURER: Maria, can you hear it? The music? It wants me to [inaudible] the eye.

[Comment: Agent Murer laughing. Transcriber notes no discernible "music."]

MURER: Are you inside the circle?

[Comment: Unidentifiable birdcalls at excess volume. Probably a large flock.]

MURER: Red. Brilliant red. Oooooooohhhh, they want my red, Maria. They can have it.

[Comment: Whimpering, as if in pain.]

MURER: Here you go, my love. It's all for you.

[Comment: Agent Murer laughs. Laughter becomes wail. Device likely dropped.]

MURER: It's so beautiful…

[Comment: Recording continues for seven hours twenty-three minutes. Sounds of rain and wildlife. Birdsong. No further content.]

ISAAC MENUZA is part of the machine. Don't trust him. His stories of family life with his wife and three children in northern Virginia are completely fabricated. Avoid his iniquitous scribblings in Punk Noir Magazine, Ghost Orchid Press, Hellhound Magazine, and Black Hare Press. Certainly don't follow him on Twitter @Imenuza, or at his website, www.isaacmenuza.com. You've been warned.

PANDORA MOTH

Freydís Moon

the Pandora Moth returns to their homeland every twenty-four months

gray and mauve bodies fixed with   wings / antennae / setae   stain the high desert

suck the life from—

    ponderosa

    longpine

and wobble across sidewalks, cling to doorframes, perch on streetlamps

welcoming their predetermined death like sluggish ballerinas

because the Pandora Moth has been buried here already

beneath those ponderosas; those longpines

and burst from their pupae ready to   fly / devour / end

their elegant corpses

     crushed under designer boots

     spread across hot asphalt

     plummet from the sky

the forestry project calls them: outbreak

like something unnatural and uncontained

and i wonder what they'll say—those scientists, those experts

when the Pandora Moth begins to listen

    oh, our poor ponderosas, they'll hear

    oh, our leeched longpines, they'll hear

and in twenty-four months a pupae will crack open between   second and third rib

                                                        tailbone and vertebrae

                                                        where wrist meets hand

the Pandora Moth will crawl down a throat and say *oh, tree*

the Pandora Moth will push outward and emerge from   cuticles

                                                        eyesockets

                                                        gums

the Pandora Moth will return to their homeland

for their   birth / funeral / reanimation

    and they'll call us home

FREYDÍS MOON (they/them) is a biracial nonbinary writer, tarot reader, and tasseographist. When they aren't writing or divining, Freydís is usually trying their hand at a recommended recipe, practicing a new language, or browsing their local bookstore. They are on Twitter @freydis_moon

THORNS ARE MEANT TO PRICK THE HEART OF SINNERS

Keely O'Shaughnessy

The roses became a fixture after Daddy disappeared. Scathing late night whispers exchanged for endless digging, planting, and pruning.

And now, the stench of boiling bones seeps into every pore of our house, but it's thickest in the kitchen, where mother has three pots bubbling away for bonemeal. Sweet, sickly steam rises and clings to the ceiling.

At her feet, there's a fresh thicket of roses she's yet to plant. Roots submerged in water; a thorny crown of stems twists upwards. She steps over them to greet me,the thorns snagging her skirt.

"Good day?" she asks. A line of blood is drawn from her calf to her ankle.

Before I have a chance to answer, her attention drifts back to her roses, back to the bones she'll cook until almost jelly. The bones that, once dried out, she'll grind to powder.

The following day, she moves from bones to wilted blooms for rosewater, which she'll wear daubed on her wrists and neck. Scent bottles with ornate stoppers join the jars of fresh bone dust on the countertop. The ground bone separates into layers of ochre and grey, and at the bottom, where larger shards have settled, there's a glimmer of something else. I reshuffle them as I watch her, twisting the jars this way and that, so the metallic flecks catch the light like Daddy's polished class ring.

All the while, Mother presses pulped petals through wire mesh, and hums as the pungent liquor seeps into the bowl beneath. Her flesh is dyed a deep, scalded pink.

I want to ask about Daddy. If he's lost and can't find his way home. If he's with that woman from his work, Marline, who mother says is too old to wear cherry brandy coloured lipstick and skirts that hug her hips.

Instead, I say, "The oldest living rose is a thousand years old."

She won't look at me because I have Daddy's features, his sharp chin, his high cheek bones.

"It's at Hildesheim Cathedral in Germany," I continue, but her gaze stays firmly fixed on the mass of congealed petals in front of her. And I wonder what it is that the roses say to her. What they whisper; what they offer her as she sings to them. What secrets they keep hidden. What it takes to keep living for a thousand years.

"Mother nature is special," I say.

That evening, I take a jar of bonemeal from the kitchen and follow mother into the garden. She digs with her hands like an animal, and, fingers scratching in the earth, she buries the millipede roots of a Black Baccara. Then, a sprawling, spiny dog rose whose barbs are dense and needle sharp.

I cough to announce my presence, but Mother focuses on coaxing unruly petioles around a half-rotten length of trellis.

"Where is he?" I ask, hugging the jar to my chest.

She works faster then, arching stems and coiling them tight against the latticework. Thorns lacerating her hands and arms.

I watch her skin turning red. "Tell me."

She opens her mouth to speak, and I sigh, imagining that she'll tell me he'll be back soon with candies and a dozen sweetheart roses wrapped in tissue paper. And that I'd be shocked by any other answer.

"He's likely just cooling off somewhere," she says, finally.

When I raise the jar above my head, Mother's mouth is a perfect, gaping oval. She stretches her bloodied arm to stop me, but it's too late. Glass fizzes like fireworks, and gritty plumes of bonemeal choke the air. Mother clamps her hands across her mouth and nose so that she doesn't inhale the particles of Daddy and Marline that swirl around us, whereas I tilt my head skywards and stick out my tongue.

Awaiting the taste of iron, dirt and a putrefied sweetness thorns rupture along my spine, and dusky, cherry-brandy buds blossom from my throat.

I'm the Hildesheim rose that still clings to crumbling cathedral walls. The rose that's flourished while all about have died. The rose that continues to feast on the ashes of the lost, and whose job it is to condemn the wicked. And Mother knows her fate is set.

KEELY O'SHAUGHNESSY (she/her) is a fiction writer with Cerebral Palsy, who lives in Gloucestershire, U.K. She has writing forthcoming in Bath Flash Fiction Award *and* Emerge Literary Journal. *She has been published* with Ellipsis Zine, NFFD, Complete Sentence, *and* Reflex Press, among others. When not writing, she likes discussing David Bowie with her cat. Find her at keelyoshaughnessy.com*

THE DEVIL'S GILLS

Maggie D. Brace

Spore by spore it began. Slowly and silently, the rich substrata of soil beneath our feet had been producing and harboring a monstrosity. Scientists were still debating how the fungus could have adapted so quickly. Of course there were conspiracy theories, finger pointing, and posturing, but no one knew exactly how or where this excrescence of flora had begun. As an authority on botany, I had been called in to opine by local government agencies, but I had little idea just what a task lay before me.

My graduate research centered on nyctinasty. In a nutshell, it covered the nastic movement of higher plants in response to the onset of darkness—essentially, the closing of the flower's petals. Well, fungi were definitely not a higher plant, and intrinsically had no petals to close. This conundrum befuddled us for quite a while, but the continued growth by leaps and bounds was so alarming, we weren't exactly sure just what we were dealing with.

As a first step, a mixture of potassium bicarbonate was administered, which provided us with the horrifying realization of what type of enemy we were confronting. Instead of killing off the growth as usual, the fungus seemed to slurp the poisonous concoction in and slowly broadcast it back out into the air. When a stronger, more lethal mixture was applied, it was as if the fungus had adapted and developed an immunity to any level of fungicide we could attack it with. It was almost as if it had used our initial dose to create its own vaccine, counteracting the poison's effect on it.

This chilling thought gave rise to a new calculation about the actual size of the growth. It had originally been thought it was limited to the Surrey area and the surrounding countryside. However, reports began to pour in identifying offshoots of the fungus in nearly every county. A team of scientists, local constabulary, greenhouse workers, and volunteer grad students were sent out to verify the reports and procure samples.

Taking samples presented a new twist to this already bizarre turn of events. The fungus appeared to have developed a means of mobility unheard of before. As the core sample tests were being conducted, the fungus seemed to simply move away from whatever trowel, shovel, pipe, or hand was sent in to extricate it. If we dug to the left, it moved to the right. If we dug down two feet, it lingered three feet below us. The implausibility of such a thing was astonishing. This strange growth was already demonstrating a higher level of thinking, one that had never been recorded in plants before.

As hours turned into days, the spectrum of our investigation turned from the original question of "What the bloody hell is this thing?" to "Will mankind survive?" The British Army had stationed themselves at ground zero, keeping all civilians away and limiting scientists' exposure to it. They were concocting various armaments, and bombarding it with everything they could think of short of nuclear arms.

In my opinion, this was the turning point in our battle with 'Freddy the Fun Guy', as some newspapers had dubbed the massive growth. I personally always thought about the growth as feminine in nature, no doubt due to its unparalleled fecundity, but Freida the Fun Guy just didn't have the same ring to it. No longer willing to be beset upon by England's finest, Freddy began to retaliate.

At first it was little things like the ground opening up under armored tanks and other vehicles, swallowing them up into some sort of sinkhole. Then it moved on to a different tactic. Enormous fruiting bodies began appearing around tents, encapsulating entire regiments in an impenetrable tangle of mycelium.

Hypothesizing that in the areas where Freddy was not being assailed, he remained quietly underground, I put forth a cease fire postulation. This was met with the expected harrumphs and grumbles from the military, but eventually was given the green light and enforced. Needless to say, the encased tents and entombed vehicles slowly reappeared, with little or no apparent harm done. Freddy had won this battle.

Spring boarding off my previous hypothesis, I conjectured there might be a way to communicate with Freddy. Linguists, botanists, and musicians joined ranks, experimenting with a variety of sounds and rhythms, trying to unlock the hidden language of fungi. While slight inroads were made in this area, a great hue and cry began, led by conservationists, to leave the poor fungus alone.

Perhaps it was inevitable, but this was the turning point in the slow procession of our understanding Freddy. We hadn't really ever looked at it from his perspective. We merely saw an anomaly and strove to eradicate it. Freddy had exhibited more and more intelligence with everything we threw at him. It almost seemed that he was becoming more humanlike as we grew more savage. Freddy was becoming a sentient creature before our very eyes, and rather than appreciate him for what he had become, we simply wanted him to go back to being a simple organism again.

While the world seemed torn about how to deal with the ever-increasing mass beneath us, Freddy seemed to gather himself and take further strides to demonstrate his power. Church graveyards became his next avenue of interest. When I learned of this novelty, my heart skipped a beat and, perhaps for the very first time, I tried to put myself in Freddy's mindset. What could he possibly want with deceased corpses slowly decaying and moldering away beneath the earth's surface? What about a ready-made host to do his bidding?

Almost unable to utter my deepest, darkest fears, I eventually made my most bizarre hypothesis to date, which was, unfortunately, also my last. That night, Freddy unleashed upon the world his army of death. From every casket, from every shire, from coast to coast, a ghoulish horde of fungus soldiers ascended. His patchwork of fungus, decay, and corpse knitted together to take over the world. As each living creature was encountered, be it man or beast, it was slowly encased in a stenchful sludge, sucked into the mire, and assimilated into the new and improved Freddy.

MAGGIE D BRACE, a life-long denizen of Maryland, teacher, gardener, basketball player and author attended St. Mary's College, where she met her soulmate, and Loyola University, Maryland. She has written 'Tis Himself: The Tale of Finn MacCool and Grammy's Glasses, *and has multiple short works and poems in various anthologies. She remains a humble scrivener and avid reader.*

THE BALETE TREES WERE THE FIRST TO RISE

Lerah Mae Barcenilla

The balete trees were the first to rise, rise, rise
>until their canopies covered the sky, gnarled fingers reaching

for each other. The stars were the second to disappear, blinking
>behind rustling leaves as the ground took her last

breath. There was a word in our dialect that meant to unravel, to break
>apart and when the land trembled, she summoned the last

remnants of our ancestors' magic. Some said the pulse was so strong it called
>the trees up, up, up until the sun was but a sliver

in the sky. There was a word in our dialect that meant to bloom, like flowers
>uncurling petal by petal by petal, old magic drawing

itself into a cocoon, the ancient land crackling under all its power until one
>day something stronger can grow out of its ashes.

LERAH MAE BARCENILLA is a poet and writer who grew up in a small town called Cuartero in the Philippines full of magic, tradition and superstition. Bearing the two halves of her parents' names, Lerah writes about memory, mythology, folklore and the state of duality. She particularly enjoys breaking apart narrative structures and exploring how words exist on and outside of the page. You can find her on Twitter as @l_erah, or Instagram @l.erah.

KUDZU

Danielle Davis

The vines were everywhere. Long, fat tendrils snaked in loops from the trees and twisted down the length of the trunks. They wrapped around the electrical poles and the swooping wires. It was a thick mass of greenery that lined the side of the road for as far as they could see.

"Kudzu, man," Jeremy told Trista. "Welcome to the south."

She eyed it distastefully. "Where does it end?"

"It doesn't." Jeremy raised his eyebrows as he looked at her gravely. "They say you can hear it growing, like corn. Two inches an hour."

"That isn't possible," Trista said. "Is it?"

Jeremy just grinned.

Their truck, Jeremy's trusted F150, had broken down on the long stretch of Highway 60. When smoke began billowing from underneath the hood, Jeremy cursed.

"Do you have cell service out here?" he asked.

Trista checked her phone. "No."

Jeremy cursed again. "I supposed we'll have to wait for someone to come along." They both cast a look down the highway, watching the summer heat shimmer like waves over the pavement in the distance.

"How long will that be?"

Jeremy suppressed a sigh of annoyance. They had been dating for three months and this road trip was supposed to be a weekend trip, a way for them to bond over miles of adventure as they traveled from Franklin, Tennessee down to the "world famous" Flea Market in Pine Bluff, Arkansas. But so far, all he'd done was get annoyed at her stupid questions. And now his baby was sick.

He stroked a hand over the hood and frowned. "No telling. But I'm sure it won't be long. This is a main thoroughfare. And I'm sure someone has the number of a tow truck. It's just a matter of time."

But that had been two hours ago. With the AC out, even having the windows down barely generated much of a cross-through breeze.

"It's, like, a thousand degrees out here," Trista said, as she fanned herself with an oil change receipt she'd found in the floorboard of the truck. Jeremy eyed her. Beads of sweat dotted her chest like small pearls, giving her a dew-kissed look that he found rather appealing. Once he got past the disheveled tendrils of hair that were plastered to her forehead, thatwas.

"It's Arkansas, babe. In the summer. Did you expect snow?"

She glared at him and fanned herself harder. "I didn't expect to be stranded in this metal box for two hours."

"You're welcome to sit in the truck bed," he offered, a tinge of irritation leaking into his voice. If she heard it, she didn't respond, just sat back and stared with blank eyes into the distance.

Then she sat up and pointed. "Babe. BABE! There's a truck! In the distance!"

Jeremy looked. Sure enough, a produce truck was headed their way from the opposite side of the highway. They could see the tall sides of the wood slats that lined either side of the truck bed. They got out of the F150 and stepped near the hood, waving their arms in the air.

As the truck pulled even with them, Jeremy saw two men inside. One was in a dingy white undershirt and green John Deere ballcap. Behind the wheel, the other, a bald man with a long white mustache that dripped down either side of his face, merely wore a pair of jean overalls. His sweaty pink arms were well-muscled and glared in the heat.

"You kids need help?" the driver asked. For a moment, Jeremy's ears couldn't process the words through the accent. The man had pronounced "help" like "hailp," drawled so that it almost sounded like a two-syllable word.

He stepped up to the driver-side door and nodded at his truck. "Our truck broke down."

The men in the truck squinted at them in the glare of the sun but didn't say anything.

Jeremy glanced from one to the other. "Can you help us?"

"We c'n give ya a ride," the man with the ballcap answered negligently. The driver nodded and jerked his chin to indicate the back of the truck. Jeremy didn't like the way the men eyed Trista, like they were looking at a choice piece of meat on a plate.

Then he mentally shook himself. *If it helps us get to civilization again, what does it hurt?*

"Babe?" he asked, turning to look at Trista. She had remained near his truck and eyed them with open distrust.

"I don't know," she said softly. "Can we talk about it?"

A door slammed. Jeremy turned to see the man with the ballcap moving around the hood of the truck. He stepped between Jeremy and Trista, in the middle of the road, and hooked his fingers through the pockets of his jeans. His feet were hidden in scuffed leather workboots.

"Makes no difference to us," the man drawled. "But we ain't got all day to wait."

A deep sense of unease rolled through Jeremy. He didn't like the way the man had moved between them, as if trying to intimidate an answer from him. And he didn't like the way Trista kept glancing nervously back to his stalled truck.

"On second thought," Jeremy said in what he hoped was a nonchalant tone, "we'll wait. We've got a tow-truck on the way," he lied. "They should be here soon to sort us out. Thanks for the help, though." He smiled and knew it was a poor showing.

The man in the ballcap looked over his shoulder at the bald man. "Tommy? What do you think? Think these kids're safe out here waiting?"

"Awful hot out here," Tommy said. "Probably not a good idea. This kinda heat's dangerous."

Jeremy turned with an angry retort on the tip of his tongue. He wasn't about to be intimidated into going with these two yokels just because he was in a tight spot, and he sure as hell didn't trust them to take him and Trista somewhere safe.

"Thanks but no—"

He barely had time to register the gun. The bullet ripped through his left eye and blew a hole the size of a softball through the back of his head. Blood splattered in a fine red mist as bits of bone and brain riddled the street in a sheet of crimson gore.

The second bullet struck Trista in the cheekbone. She screamed, a high shriek that echoed off the woods behind her. She clapped a hand to her face and reeled backwards. The next shot got her in the back of the head and she pitched face-first into the edge of the kudzu brush.

"Mighty fine truck," Tommy said to his friend. "Should get some good parts offa it." He opened the door from the outside handle and lumbered out of the truck.

"A little warning would've been nice!" the man with the ballcap said. "You almost got me with that first one!"

Tommy waved a hand dismissively. "You were fine, Martin," he scoffed. "I am an excellent shot." He grinned. After a moment, Martin grinned back at him.

They riffled through Jeremy's pockets and pulled out his wallet. Tommy pulled out the money and split it between the two of them.

Then they snagged Trista's purse from the floorboard of the truck and snagged the cash in her wallet, as well.

Without a word between them, the men grabbed the arms and legs of each body and tossed them one-by-one into the thicket of kudzu that lined the road. As they watched, the kudzu began to move, shifting and creeping over the bodies until the brush covered every trace that they were there. Small vines slithered from the shoulder into the road to soak the leaves into the blood pooling on the asphalt. The leaves became wet and coated in a matter of minutes, the dark green turning black and shiny, then the vines slid back into the thicket and disappeared.

"Handy stuff," Martin said as he surveyed their work. Aside from the bloody steaks on the asphalt, it was just another abandoned truck on the side of the road.

"We'll come back for that later," Tommy said. "Let's get in. It's hot out."

"Dangerous kinda heat," Martin agreed. He cast a nervous glance at the kudzu, then got into the truck.

The truck rumbled as Tommy started it up, then pulled off the shoulder and drove on. Behind him, a slight breeze kicked up, sifting through the kudzu leaves like a lover's fingers. *Goodbye*, it seemed to say. *Goodbye.*

DANIELLE DAVIS's horror and dark fantasy have most recently appeared in Andromeda Spaceways Magazine, The Astounding Outpost, *and multiple anthologies. She is a bisexual author writing through a Bi-Polar Disorder lens. You can find her on most social media under the handle "LiteraryEllyMay" and at www.literaryellymay.com.*

BRITTLE IS THE BARK
THAT CRIES

Nikki R. Leigh

When the white spots appeared under their nails, the Gibbons family brushed it off. Their fingertips glimmered, a picture of health, save for the white shapes no more than the size of a comma on a keyboard, dancing through the veneer of their nails.

"I bet it's from pinching my fingers under the rolling pin the other day," Ma Gibbons said.

Papa Gibbons eyed his own nails. "Just a mineral deficiency. Haven't been eating right with all this work."

"Worms!" Baby Gibbons shrieked, surprising both Ma and Papa with her linguistic achievements at the age of two.

The family said nothing as they tilled the fields near the woods—those dreadful woods where fire had raged not two years ago. The lines had held near the small row of homes, but the landscape reminded them of what had come so close to taking it all. Broken, burnt trees. Black and brown brush, stretched for acres across a dreary landscape.

But, as time passed, the damage faded from the terrain. Patches of dead, wiry trees stood tall to touch the stars, the only evidence of the fire's ravages. By some stroke of luck—or perhaps some microbial magic—the forest was thriving, pushing the marks of devastation further and further out as vivacious branches sprouted and advanced.

But still... those damned spots under their nails. Ma tried to rub hers away, her fingers grooming the smooth surface, trying to push the white squiggles to the edges.

"Jesus, Mary, and Joseph!"

"What's the matter?" Papa asked from his spot at the bathroom sink, splashing water on his face.

"They moved! I swear they moved."

At that moment, the tiny worms that had made their way under their nails from the soil they'd tilled woke up. They wriggled, like maggots in spoiled meat, beneath the sheet of nail, against their skin, a tenacious and unpleasant tickle.

Baby Gibbons laughed on the floor, holding her hands up and moving her fingers back and forth in the air, curling her digits and then splaying them wide.

The three flexed their fingers, trying hopelessly to dig at the itch that spread beneath their nails. Dozens of small worms, flat, white, and very much alive, continued their dance.

Ma Gibbons attempted to scratch it away. She couldn't get deep enough, so she opted to scratch… anything she could find. She dug into her arms, her chest, her thighs, hoping to get some skin beneath the nail of her finger to reach that unpleasant untouchable place. Blood welled in the wake of the abrading and nails separated from their anchor, splintering and driving the hard materials into the vulnerable skin underneath.

Pa Gibbons, always direct, reached for a screwdriver, a pair of pliers, anything he could find to get under. And, when the blunt of the tools only dug so far, he determined to remove the problematic tissue instead.

Baby Gibbons, laughter turning to tears, toddled to her feet and simply walked away. As fast as her legs would allow, she entered the woods. Her parents, too busy smashing and prying and angered at the betrayal of their hands, didn't notice the absence of her laughs and cries.

With the nearly microscopic grubs broken and released into their skin, the Gibbons felt their agency slip away, the woods whispering their suggestions and ushering them forth. Their fingernails, crushed to the quick, left a path of candied blood on their way to the woods.

Through the trees Ma and Papa walked, marching like toy soldiers, their minds unable to tell their bodies to turn back the other way. Dead leaves crunched under their feet, the soft *plopping* of blood in their wake singing their arrival to the edge of the woods.

Ma and Papa caught up to Baby Gibbons, and together they walked deeper, deeper until they found where green met brown and black, where the trees struggled to grow after the fire took its toll. They found their trees, the ones calling their names, raised their hands like claws, and scratched. The noise their fingernails made, as they raked their hands across the brittle, dry shell, echoed throughout the forest. The bark peeled back, layer by layer, to expose the broken flora for what it was: a plant in desperate need of help to survive.

The trunk tore, brown splintering under their nails.

For hours, the three toiled to erode the thick skin of the brown giant, until they had reached the pulp, sickened and gray, so close to death. Their fingers found purchase in the bloodied ruts, and there they remained, as the Gibbons stood, stock still, eyes boring straight ahead, seeing nothing.

The trees drank. Latched onto their fingers and sucked. Life drained from each body, their skin deflating, color depleting from their faces.

Suckling, nipping, their fingers but straws for the unmoving, despondent trees.

Ma Gibbons, her mind empty, had another role left in her life to fulfill: a full-time pollinator, for the rest of her days.

If Papa Gibbons could have thought, he might have wondered what good opposable thumbs do if they're glued to the trunks of trees.

Baby Gibbons, with much less life to give the trees—a sapling herself—didn't have a chance to contemplate the life she had yet to live.

Like their neighbors, their friends, the strangers that passed through the land, the Gibbons became nothing more than a pile of skin and bones at the bases of the trees. They'd seep into the soil, drain through the forest as they decomposed, and provide one more gift for the earth: a happy home for infinitesimal hordes of white worms to find their next host, a calling card for the wonders of nature they served.

NIKKI R. LEIGH is a queer, forever-90s-kid wallowing in all things horror. When not writing horror fiction and poetry, she can be found creating custom horror-inspired toys, making comics, and hunting vintage paperbacks. She reads her stories to her partner and her cat, one of which gets scared very easily.

Instagram - @spinetinglers
Twitter - @fivexxfive
Email – spinetinglersmedia@gmail.com

HANDPRINTS

Lucas Carroll-Garrett

Rust-orange clay crunched under his hiking boots and the unstoppered sun reminded Rechierre of how pale his skin was. Working from an air-conditioned lab down in Tananarive had done nothing for his fitness. Soon he was panting, but he had to hurry. They had found human bones at the dig site.

He leaned against one of the bleached tree trunks that dotted the surrounding wasteland, sweat running down his fingers to turn the whitened wood surly grey. Central Madagascar swelled before him, a sticky looking expanse of equatorial clay dotted with green. Jungle still clung to the mountainsides like spots of mold, despite the farmers' best efforts. The nearest swathe of trees was smoking—more farms being set up.

Rechierre squinted through the haze to pick out the corrugated metal shed, their forward base. Dr. Chambeau peeked his head past the already rusting doorway and waved him in. The big man's easy grin bared white against his deep tan, his eyes glinted a wild green with excitement. Inside, he slammed a burly elbow onto the folding table that was the shed's centerpiece and held up a ridge of bone. "Recognize this?" he almost laughed.

Keeping his own delicate hands folded in his lap, Rechierre leaned forward to inspect it: a brown and brittle jawbone, curving gently around the man's thumb. The teeth were cracked and worn by now, but it was impossible not to recognize that death's-head grin.

"Lower mandible," he said. "Human."

Dr. Chambeau's own grin widened, showing the translucent pink of his gums.

"Not quite, kid. Look: Two Mental Foramina. We only have one." His finger tapped manically between two small holes in the bone, right where the jawline broke off. "We've got a new species on our hands."

The breath left Rechierre's body. "You're sure?"

"Ninety percent. But that's why you're here." He placed the jaw delicately back into its padded box. "DNA analysis will give our paper an edge, might even tell us what happened to these people."

Rechierre eyed the box's worn edges and tried to still his beating heart. Sure, the cave was old, but... "There were no people on Madagascar until a couple thousand years ago. This group predates the indigenous population?"

The man's lips closed around his teeth, making his grin smug.

"By a long shot. No one else has been inside for a hundred thousand years. We've got special access from the government. Hell, no one even knew the cave was here until they cleared the trees out. So, kid? You want a look?"

Rechierre didn't need to say anything. His expression was enough. Laughing, Dr. Chambeau put an arm over his shoulder and led him to the jagged split in the mountainside. The white crags against the gaping blackness reminded Rechierre of the open-mouthed sharks swimming around in the capitol's aquarium.

The doctor stuck his head inside and Rechierre followed suit, bent double. The musk of turned earth hit him as the cave's cool air curled around his sweaty skin. The space was broad and flat, stretching back into the murk for about the length of a tennis court. A faint breeze tugged Rechierre's hair back towards the outside.

"Nice place, huh? Dusty but spacious. Enough for several families." Dr. Chambeau groped along the garish yellow extension cord that ran through the undisturbed dirt until he found the standing lamp. "Makes you wonder why the folks here didn't spread, colonize the whole island."

He clicked the lamp on, lighting a small block of neatly excavated dirt outlined in a square of string marked with coordinate tags. Behind it rose a wall of the same pale stone as the entrance, painted with hundreds of handprints. Rechierre had seen similar patterns in France's Ice Age sites, splayed hands of long-dead ancestors outlined in pigment. Here, the hands layered over each other, stretching up into the dark that the lamp couldn't reach.

Rechierre hugged his thin arms around his white button-up. He didn't belong in here. It was someone else's home. He stretched his hand out to one of the prints and found that the fingers were stubby and spaced out differently than his own. A different species...

No, some*thing* else's home. No human had ever lived here.

Dr. Chambeau loomed behind him, arm outstretched.

"Your soil samples." The lamp cast his heavy features in a thick shadow, especially the rictus of his grin. "Sorry to make you tramp all the way out here, but I'm the only crew until Tuesday. Come back next week, see if we can't find some more bones for you to ogle."

Unsure if he ever wanted to come back to such a place, Rechierre sneezed dust out his nose, mumbled some sort of promise, and grabbed the baggies of dirt with shivering fingers. He had never been so glad to step out into the swelter of the island's shadeless sun.

Back in his pristine white lab, Rechierre rested with his head next to the air-conditioner in the windowsill. He had felt queasy ever since the cave, but his flu test had come back negative. So he spent the week running bits of soil through batteries of tests. It was the usual over-watered equatorial clay, though rich in organic material and iron content. He had heard of iron correlating with bone middens where hominids would butcher animals, but the samples were supposed to be from all across the cave. He rubbed at his throbbing temples. Where had the blood come from?

He had just managed to isolate some hominid DNA amidst the prey animals and curious abundance of bacterial DNA when his phone buzzed:

Kid. Get over here. Crew found another room. Complete skeletons.

Curiosity overcame Rechierre's queasiness and he ran for the bus station, the cave's chill forgotten. *Skeletons*, plural. Most sites would be lucky to produce a complete fingerbone! This time he arrived completely out of breath, sprinting across the no man's land outside. Dr. Chambeau's arm stuck out of the dark crack in the hillside, waving him in again.

He led Rechierre along the handprint-infested wall to where the ceiling sloped to meet the cave floor. A thin crack spiderwebbed through the rock, widening just enough for a human at the base.

"After you." The doctor coughed. "Crew says they're not feeling well today, milking those paid sick days. Just the two of us."

By now the cave's chill had seeped back into Rechierre's sweat-damp clothes, and when tried to squeeze through, the layers of dust stuck to him. The stuff went up his throat, making him cough too as the rock dug into him. It made his headache worse.

Rechierre gave one last heave and pulled himself into the open. Unsure how high the ceiling was in the gloom, he switched his flashlight on before standing up.

A skull's grin greeted him, sitting neatly amongst a scatter of ribs. Rechierre jumped back involuntarily, scraping his head on rock. He managed a deep breath and swept the beam around the cave. Thirteen skeletons lay in a semicircle around him, each huddled up against the wall of the round chamber. On his knees, he shuffled into the center to get a better look and make room for Dr. Chambeau, still coughing behind him.

The dust swirled thick around him, stinging his squinting eyes. Each skeleton was in remarkable condition, bones a deep chocolate brown, slightly stouter than a *Homo sapiens*.

"These really—ahem—do look like separate species," he called out into the dark. Dr. Chambeau started to agree but was overcome by a particularly violent coughing fit.

Remarkably, each individual seemed to be young, no signs of arthritis or pre-mortem injuries. Yet they were all dead in the back of this cave. Why? He swept his flashlight about and found a splash of red behind him.

The handprints continued along the cave wall. But in here, each print was almost obscured by a spray of red ochre, still vibrant after all these millennia. "Doctor? What do you make of this?"

The silence was broken only by his own cough.

"Doctor?" he asked again, his voice rising in pitch.

Shuffling over to where the big man was still halfway out of the narrow passage, Rechiere shook the meat of his shoulder. Dr. Chambeau's head lolled, staring up at him with blank, dead eyes, his mouth lined in red blood.

Half-screaming and half-coughing, Rechierre scrambled back, dropping his flashlight. He retreated too far into the dark, and bones bit into his scrabbling fingers. He snatched them back, huddling in the center of the room and clutching his spinning head, trying to figure out what had happened. He gave one final, deep cough and his hand came away sticky. He looked at the healthy pile of bones beside him, then at the stained hands along the wall, head pounding worse than ever. Slowly, he edged his own hand into the beam of light. His palm was covered by a splash of red.

From the hills of Tennessee, LUCAS CARROLL-GARRETT is a new writer interested in the relationship between humanity and nature, and between the mundane and fantastical. After studying Biology, he pivoted to storytelling and is working towards an MFA in Creative Writing. His work recently won runner-up for the Mike Resnick Memorial Award.

NIGHT GINKGOES

Jennifer Shneiderman

Tree failure they call it

ginkgo leaves quiver in indignation

light dims over swaths of Blackstone Square

sunset signals the leaves

lift away in unison from gnarled, outstretched branches

fly ginkgo leaf-bats fly

take wing over the South End

Tree failure they call it

the ginkgoes make their counts

15-20% of the freshly planted

die in their first year

withering from heat and negligence

dying of thirst

trees could save humans from a barren future

but humans are busy building, using

laying waste as

the temperature and waters rise

Tree failure they call it
ginkgo leaves gather against gentrified windows
rolling and whispering
sliding down concrete walkways
the developer takes the stairs
slips on wet, fan-shaped leaves
out of nowhere
the stairs take the developer

Tree failure they call it
more ginkgo leaves swoop
plastering a construction truck windshield
red lights spin
red blood spills
leaves peel off shattered glass
go into formation
speeding to their trees
returning to posts before dawn

Tree failure they call it
deceptive in their innocent, beguiling butterfly shape
ginkgoes tremble in anticipation
they breathe deeply
they yellow

they sigh

they pretend-faint

they fall

they are ready

JENNIFER SHNEIDERMAN is a Licensed Clinical Social Worker living in Los Angeles. Her work has appeared, or is forthcoming, in many publications, including: The Rubbertop Review, Anti-Heroin Chic, The Chamber, Prospectus *and* The Perch. *She received an Honorable Mention in the Laura Riding Jackson 2020 Poetry Competition.*

THE RED SEA

G.B. Lindsey

It's a gorgeous day. The beach is oily and red.

The girl draws a deep, deep breath. The air is thick, corroding iron. A thousand seagulls eddy above; their screeches fill her ears to the top and overflow. She hears other shrieks, on chuckles, on guffaws. The roll of the waves is a thumping tympani.

She walks through sucking sand toward a man wearing a straw hat. There is a feather on it—peacock blue—and the brim is as wide as a sombrero's. He is talking—to her? There's no one else near. He tells her the beach is rare, sand like this "only comes from around here, see how it changes color from blonde to brunette to auburn. Down by the water, down there on the edge, see? It's as dark as wine."

He's right. She walks down to get a better view.

The sand near the swell squeezes through her toes, chunky-warm. Pink water bubbles up in the dents she leaves behind. The girl looks over her shoulder and watches the pools seep back out of sight.

She wants to wash her feet but the water doesn't look clear today.

The people already in the waves don't care. They laugh louder than the seagulls scream. Children shriek and jump, fathers throw their daughters in the air and the daughters splash down in ripe gushes of brine. The daughters' suits are all the color of cherries—Bing cherries, sour cherries, chokecherries. Their hair is plastered to their foreheads and necks like strings of skin. The girl shades her eyes and watches two women sculling chest-deep, rising and sinking in the swell. They chat and nod and smile, wiping hair from their faces again and again.

"Part," the girl says, pointing a finger at the sea. She does not know why, only that it must be said. The water does not part. Brown foam crests the next wave and drags back, streaking the beach. It swallows her ankles, paints her toes, softens her footprints into vague pocks.

"Part."

The sea does not listen.

"It's a nice beach." That man waves from way back where the sand is dry, but his voice has ventured closer, right at her ear. "Watch out for jellyfish."

They squish under the soles of her feet. Plop, slip. Watermelon Jell-O, wobbly and toxic. A little boy balances on one leg, unknotting a tentacle from between his toes. His shorts drip in rivulets down his calves. The tentacle keeps coming as he pulls, longer and longer, an endless ephemeral rope. The sky is green. Yellow and purple, too; the sun drapes a veil over its face, and everything is orange as embers.

"There's no lifeguard," she warns. The people laugh and wave, and fins break the surface like winking eyes. The boy winds and winds the tentacle around his wrist.

She scrunches wet sand between her toes. It's very warm.

"Come in, you!" A female voice. The girl squints. A woman bounces in the waves, middle-aged, wearing a purple-red racing suit with skinny straps. "We'll swim out! See the seals."

The girl tastes grit in her teeth, and salt, and ash. The woman in the waves flails her hands about, claps and barks like a seal. A shark as long as a van slides past, baring pearl teeth above the surface. Sooty top, star-white belly.

"You stupid, stupid woman," the girl calls back. She cups her mouth and calls again, and this time the wind does not steal it away. The woman laughs and the shark rolls back on the wave with her left arm in its mouth. The patch of water around the woman turns black. The smell is horrific.

"Just out there," the woman says, and cranks her shoulder back as though her arm were still attached. "Seals!"

The woman sinks down in a funnel of blood. Her eyes grin once before submerging.

The girl sees islands far out in the haze, glass poking in a jagged line toward the sky. Birds cloud around them like midges, great amorphous screaming blots above dark spires. The ocean crests across the girl's toes; the tide is coming in. Each wave opens like a grave, each trough is a cavern. The children jump into them, into the red sea, into maws that gape, between fences of teeth. A father throws his daughter up. The daughter splashes down in a circle of black wedges. They tighten. Tighten.

Then the girl is in the water, up to her thighs. It's too warm, a brackish bathtub full of hair-dye. Lost things bump against her legs, fingers and toes and noses. She stares up at the beach, at the spike of the island, at the birds in a grimy cloud, at the man in the straw hat with the feather, a winking speck of blue. Water hisses out, sucks at her legs as though it, too, knows the path must be cleared, the waters must part.

The ocean roars behind her and she looks back.

Surfer's wave is coming. Surfer gnashes white teeth and rears his huge grey head and stares out of eyes bottomless and black. Surfer slides on his belly, graceful as a dolphin along the swell's curve.

"Walk faster," the girl orders. Her legs slog through the sea, searching for a path, but the sand caves away beneath her feet and the water is heavy, leaning against her thighs. Just behind, Surfer's jaws meet with a heavy whump. The wind whistles Amazing Grace through his teeth.

She walks, and the wave gains.

Fingers find her wrist, curling like worms, and the woman with one arm floats by, hair trailing. Dark hair, ending where the sea begins. The woman smiles upward. She is the girl's mother. Her face is painted, ashen skin caked in stage makeup. It cracks and splinters around her mouth. Her fingers are stiff and the sun shines off her teeth, glimmers in filmy blue eyes, once as blue as that feather.

The girl squints. "You're dead. You're dead, go away from me."

"Lead us out," her mother says from four feet away. The missing arm sloshes in the surf, steel fingers wrapping tighter and tighter around the girl's wrist. "Lead us out of hell."

"This isn't hell." She turns and looks Surfer in the teeth. "This isn't hell."

But she doesn't believe.

G.B. LINDSEY's most salacious and long-term affair is with the horror genre, but she also writes sci-fi, romance, and historical fiction. By day, she works in kidney transplant; by night she reads voraciously and devours period dramas. You can find her other works at www.gblindsey.com.

CHRYSANTHEMUM

Victoria Audley

Jonquil did not care for conversing in words. She found them too small, too insufficient for the emotion she wished to convey with them. Her words never seemed to come out right, and the frustration was so great, she rarely bothered to try at all.

She wished she were her namesake, the flower. Free of the constraints of spoken word, plants express themselves through action: to wilt if they are thirsty, to burn if the sun is too hot. It was a language in which she was delighted to find herself able to reply: to water or to move out of the sun, to show understanding and compassion and love.

Beyond the simple communications of basic needs, she discovered that, when her plants trusted her, they began to tell her more. She was far from the first to uncover this—books full of the secret language of flowers had come into fashion years earlier—but she did not need lists written by human hands to learn the hidden truths of her plants.

The pink larkspur, cheeky and inconstant, was fickleness. The hundred-leaved rose, regal and imposing with its head held high, was pride. Some of them were more complex, like the passionate European sweetbrier's desperate declaration, "I wound to heal." The earnest yellow jonquil, of course, she intuited immediately: "I desire a return of affection."

Jonquil knew her garden inside out; she listened to the murmuring soil in harmony with the soaring, singing flowers, and watched the subtle movements of her plants, their leaves like yearning arms, reaching out for her. She chose each seed carefully, creating meaning in the arrangement of their beds. Nightshade and pansy, for clarity of mind, or Christmas rose and olive trees, for peace and tranquility. There was no more perfect joy in the world to her than the kind companionship of the friends she chose.

It was surprising, then, to one day see a flower she did not remember planting. In the back corner of the garden, tucked behind the red hand-flower trees, was a bush with bright pink flowers. It was a surprising shade, so vibrant and powerful she almost winced to look at it. Though she had not invited it, she saw the beauty and strength in it, and was curious enough to welcome the new arrival. Kneeling beside it, she reached for its petals. Suddenly, a sour note flushed through her, chilling her to the bone despite the bright morning light.

Rhododendron. "Beware."

Frowning, she rose and went to the shed. When she returned with a shovel in hand, the bush was gone. She tried to put it out of her mind, sitting amongst her moonwort and scarlet geraniums, but the memory followed her. The next day, before she looked at anything else, she returned to the corner behind the hand-flowers, but there was nothing there. She checked again the next day, and the next. She began to believe she had dreamed it, that it was a conjuration of her subconscious mind that had mistakenly crossed worlds in her memory. She planted a juniper—protection—in the back corner, and thought nothing else of it.

The day after she planted the juniper, she went to the back of the garden to check on it. The juniper was gone. In its place grew a delicate white American starwort. "A welcome stranger," it said, but Jonquil sensed something she had never felt from a plant before: dishonesty. She had always believed the messages she perceived from her plants were the pure expression of their unique identity, a signal not chosen by the plant itself, but an unconscious beacon of their inner being. Now, she began to doubt.

In terror, she sat in her garden, looking at all the plants she had nurtured and grown, wondering if she truly knew any of them at all. The globe amaranth's undying love gripped her throat with tendrils of obsession. Hydrangea, the boaster, laughed in fiery glee, daring Jonquil to best it. Indian jasmine twisted around her wrists, its amiable companionship turned in an instant to demanding imprisonment.

She spent days inside, avoiding the garden. From outside, she could hear them whispering, aching for her to return. Holding her breath, she chanced a glance out the window to the garden's back corner. Laurestina. "I die if neglected." A dark, bitter feeling rose in the back Jonquil's throat. She hoped so.

The garden erupted with rage and sorrow. Stems drooped, petals browned, leaves withered, and yet, Jonquil stayed inside. The cacophony of snapping branches and howling flowers seemed to echo off the walls around her. She locked every door, and hid herself in bed under the dark of her quilt, but still she could hear the garden screaming.

The day it fell silent did not feel like a relief. In the quiet, she could hear each beat of her heart, though it sounded as if it came from beneath the ground, through layers of soil. She walked to the door, her fingers hesitating on the doorknob, and stepped outside.

Wind whistled through the dead and rotting trees, knocking the flowers' stems together as it pushed them aside. The garden was a sea of sickly yellow, tansy and coltsfoot and birdsfoot trefoil: war, vengeance, justice.

As she made her way to the back corner, she trod on the remains of the flowers she had so lovingly raised, their decaying stems and wrinkled, bleached petals like bones beneath her feet. The garden's murmuration was a low buzz, an electric current that shocked her fingertips and coursed angrily through her nerves. In the back corner, a flash of red-violet wavered in the breeze.

Bleeding Heart. "Come with me."

The red flowers disappeared in a sudden flood of yellow. Jonquil felt thin vines wrap around her limbs and pull her down to her knees. The ground no longer felt solid; it moved constantly beneath her, as choppy as a stormy sea. She tried to scream, but no sound came out as her lungs filled with dirt.

Seemingly overnight, a garden full of roses burst forth from the grounds that had one been Jonquil's. Neighbours and passers-by were somewhat relieved by its typical beauty; much better, they all agreed, than whatever strange combinations the silent girl who once lived there put together. But for those who hear the flowers' secrets, the garden is not quite so innocuous. Of all the many bushes in the garden, there is only one kind of rose.

Maiden's Blush. "If you love me, you will find out."

VICTORIA AUDLEY escaped from a gothic novel, and after brief stints in teaching and performing, she now haunts a town by the sea. In her free time she plays too much D&D and attempts to convince the neighbourhood cats to be her friend. You can find her at https://linktr.ee/vcaudley

IMITATION OF LIFE

J.R. Handfield

My grandfather and I often hiked the wooded trails of the Pioneer Valley when I was a child. One time, we reached a clearing with a body of water, and I never forgot the giant smile on his long, angular face as he pulled an armful of purple flowers from the pond.

"Water hyacinths, my boy!" he said, his bright, blue eyes wide with joy. "Named by a poet!"

That day, my grandfather taught a course in beginner's botany to his young descendant. I learned about the roots, the stems, the spikes. I learned that water hyacinths were an invasive plant that doesn't belong in Western Massachusetts. I learned how much Gramps loved that beautiful plant straight from Greek myth.

As the sun set, my grandfather took the flowers and brought them back to the pond. I heard a sudden yelp and saw the flowers hit the ground. My grandfather shoved his thumb in his mouth and angrily waved me off with his free hand. I didn't think much more of it as we made our way home. I learned mere moments earlier that water hyacinths don't have thorns, after all.

He suffered a seizure not long after that hike. Lost his ability to speak, lost his mobility. His eyes turned a dark and distant purplish color, rarely focused on any of us.

He survived a few more years before he passed away. Fought like hell the whole time.

My mother loved telling stories about my grandfather. She would talk about the type of man he was. About his inedible meat loaf. About how much he scared her boyfriends. About his love of nature. About how he fought in Vietnam, but didn't talk about it. About all the curse words he loved to use, and how proud he looked after he uttered that first, crisp, clear, glorious "fuck" months after his seizure.

About his promise that grass would never grow at his gravesite.

My grandfather wasn't all that religious—"I'm headed either up or down whether I want to or not," he'd often say—so the idea that he could control landscaping in the afterlife... people knew better than to argue with him over something so ridiculous. More often than not, my grandmother would simply yell, "Oh, George, will you PLEASE," and playfully slap his arm. It just encouraged him more.

Still, to quote Hank Adams, chairman of the local cemetery commission, "the goddamn son of a bitch pulled it off." It's the running joke in town that ol' Georgie Greenthumb of Guerin Road finally met his match at St. Dymphna's Cemetery. My grandfather died two decades ago and, as promised, not a single blade of grass grew on that plot.

The cemetery commission tried everything to get some green stuff six feet above Gramps, but nothing worked. It remained a brown patch of dirt. When my grandmother died, years after my grandfather, we all secretly hoped the grass situation would change—maybe laying her to rest next to her husband would do the trick—that a reunion with the love of his life would prompt the grass to finally grow.

Instead, the grass grew above her casket, while his side remained barren.

We were all out of ideas. Frustrated, I decided to dress up the plot in a way that honored my relationship with Gramps: a single hyacinth bulb in a forcing jar at the foot of the headstone.

That was a mistake.

The water hyacinth is very invasive. It completely takes over once introduced to a habitat. What presents as a gorgeous green and purple plant floating upon the water is, in fact, a beautiful ecological disaster that slowly strangles its botanical brethren to death wherever it grows.

Every Tuesday afternoon, my wife and I would visit the cemetery. Rain or shine, we'd get into the car, listen to Matty B's drive-time show on WXXT-FM, set up some lawn chairs at the gravesite, crack open a couple beers, and talk to my grandparents. We'd tell them about our kids, update them on town gossip, share some off-color jokes, the usual. One Tuesday, we arrived to see that my grandmother's side of the plot was the same typical manicured grass as always. My grandfather's side, however, had transformed into a leafy carpet of green and purple, all spreading from the forcing jar. It was incomprehensible, and it was beautiful, and it was wrong—I knew I didn't plant a water hyacinth, but a regular hyacinth bulb.

The following Tuesday, we arrived to find a group of people surrounding the gravestone. The hyacinth meadow had spread past my grandfather's final resting place, across my grandmother's plot and beyond. Flowers grew almost halfway to the street and over the other plots. I moved toward the plant. The grass approaching the flowerbed was almost dewy, and the soil underneath had a little extra give to it. Inky roots spread up their headstone like a vine, organic tendrils tracing the engraved letters along its path. A flowering spike sat atop the stone on my grandfather's side; it looked like a familiar face when the light hit it at the right angle.

Without asking, I grabbed some gardening shears from a bystander. With a few quick cuts, I trimmed the hyacinths back to the boundary of the gravesite. I grabbed one bunch of cut flowers and felt a prick on my thumb. I swore and slammed the shears into the ground, the crowd going silent. What pricked me? What stung me?

The hyacinth?

I stared at my grandparent's headstone, eyeing the flowers. In spite of its strange behavior, I couldn't bring myself to cut that final, lone, defiant purple plant or destroy the first living thing to survive above my grandfather's final resting place. The idea of a reversion to the dead, lifeless brown dirt after the miracle of this plant was too much to bear.

I would come to regret it.

My phone jolted me awake on an unseasonably warm and humid Friday afternoon. It was Hank Adams of the cemetery commission.

"Jimmy, I'm sorry," he said, his voice shaking. "You need to come to George's grave. Something's up."

"What?" I asked. "Hank, I was just sleeping. I'll be back there on--."

"Dammit, just bust a hump and get down here." He hung up before I could respond.

I pulled myself out of bed and drove to the cemetery. As I turned onto the stretch of pavement where my grandparents lay, I encountered a sea of purple and green, spread across most of the road and grass. Flowers floated on a few inches of water. Headstones poked out from the impossible lake, their tops blanketed with vines and petals.

Hank stood at the edge of a road receding into an ocean in bloom. "It wasn't like this yesterday, Jimmy," he said, gesturing with an outstretched palm. "I mean, it was clearly spreading a little, but I knew you'd be down here again soon enough. This..."

The breeze picked up, rustling the leaves and petals. As the wind swirled, Hank and I watched the flowers bow toward the same central location: my grandfather's grave. The flower that snaked its way up my grandfather's headstone earlier this week from the forcing jar, the flower I couldn't bring myself to cut, was impossibly large and fully in bloom. We watched it grow and change in front of our eyes, the flowering spikes expanding and forming limbs, heads, bodies.

The air calmed, the silence broken only by the water lapping against the cemetery headstones as the waters suddenly receded. We watched the sea of plants gravitate toward the organic amalgamation of vegetation and death. Vines uprooted the earth, along with the bones and caskets and bodies of those buried below.

The flower, the meadow… it formed a head-like mass at its top. Its face was long and angular; bouquets of corpses held in its countless arms and branches. It howled, and its cry exploded in my head. I stumbled, but Hank fell to his knees and screamed. Suddenly, a dark root snapped out from the mass and decapitated him in one stroke. Before his body could hit the ground, another root wrapped itself around the headless corpse and pulled it back toward the creature's head.

The plant golem's face opened, and the monstrosity devoured Hank's carcass whole. It howled again and gazed into my eyes. I then heard my grandfather's voice reverberate within my head, my skull, my soul. I received a sudden vision of that fateful hike with my grandfather… how he pulled the plant from the water, how it pricked his finger… how it pricked my finger.

In my final moments, I finally understood. As another root whipped out from the creature, I thought back to that hike, to his funeral, to my family, to Tuesday nights. In my dying breath, his howl taught me one final lesson: how truly invasive the water hyacinth could be.

J.R. HANDFIELD (@jrhandfield on Twitter) lives in Central Massachusetts with his wife, his son, and his cat; not necessarily in that order. He is a co-editor of ProleSCARYet: Tales of Horror and Class Warfare, *and his work can be found in* Punk Noir Magazine, Hellhound Magazine, *and multiple* Hundred Word Horror *anthologies from Ghost Orchid Press.*

the interloper

Corey Niles

the rain runs around

the scabs on the trees

I pick one off

place it on my tongue

consume the scar

rub my cheek on the soft wood beneath it

wrap my arms around the broad trunk

pray for lightning to strike

burn away the cold that's consumed me since we touched down

damn this lingering cough

I won't let it isolate me any longer

purifying water

dampen me

peel off this flesh like soft bark

I surrender my body to you

make use of it

if only as fertilizer

I'm tired of being an interloper

I want to be a part of this strange place

COREY NILES was born and raised in the Rust Belt, where he garnered his love of horror. His recent and forthcoming publications include "The Crows Belonged to Me" in HWA Poetry Showcase Vol. VII, *and "What Lurks in These Woods" in* Pink Triangle Rhapsody.

TOOTH

Elecia Page

It started with a tooth.

The tooth in question, dirt flecked and ground smooth, was firmly and resolutely clasped within the fist of a young woman. She stood solidly at the edge of a deep gash in the earth. Autumn vegetation brushed at her ankles, and a cool breeze rasped across the fabric of her dress.

Before her, a large hole had been crudely and indiscriminately dug. Had her hands been held freely at her sides rather than gripped behind her back, the grime coating her nails would have clearly pointed to the tools that had scraped and scratched up the soil.

George Chester was not impressed. She could tell by the way his narrow eyes greedily searched the floor about her feet. He had not spoken a word to her on the swift trek up to the grove, nor had he condescended to look at her. She flinched when he finally spoke, his voice clear and loud like the metallic chime of church bells in dark hours.

"Where did you find it? Show me at once," he insisted.

She knelt down by the hole and gestured excitedly. "Here, sir. I searched around for the rest, but nothing yet. I am sure there is more."

"What makes you think so?"

"I—I just know."

She had no explanation for him. She had felt the tooth as if it hummed just for her to reach down and claim it. It jutted out from the surface scrub and she had plucked it as if it were a daisy. She had heard stories of great skeletal lizards pulled from the land, and the thrill of discovery had her elbows deep in the mud. She would gladly spend her days rooting around outside, and harboured a secret hope that Mr. Chester might teach her the necessary skills to locate and extract fossils. Possibly even the opportunity to carve an exit out of the relentless monotony of village life.

"That will be all," George said dismissively.

"Ah, but, sir—" she started, and was cut off just as quickly with a sharp hand raised by George.

"I said, that will be all." He extended his raised hand towards her, palm facing the sky. His hand was pale and smooth, more suited to the softness of a glove than the weathering of hard labour. She was still for a moment before understanding that he waited for the tooth. Cursing inwardly, she dropped it into his palm. It was over as quickly as it began.

George wasted no time in rushing back to seek the help of a handful of young men to carry his tools from his accommodation to the dig site. He was turned around a few times on the journey, and lost the path to tall grass and thick brambles. Eventually, he emerged from the woods and followed a rust-tinted river back to the village. All those he accosted shook their heads and advised him against his enterprise. *Busy, sir,* and even one whisper that sounded like *no chance.*

George arrived at his room after dark in a foul temper, frustrated and baffled at the reluctance of the villagers. He'd even waved his coin purse around to absolutely no avail. He kicked his tool bag across the room. The tools that spilled onto the floorboards were clean and bright, unused for many years after George had realised that his talents as an archaeologist leaned towards the buying and selling of other people's finds rather than the unearthing of his own. Weeks could pass here before he found anything worthwhile.

Weeks did pass. George went to bed each night tired and aching, after toiling away alone at the site. A stubborn will not to return empty handed drove his shovel swing each day, and his hard work was paid off by an almost full set of teeth. He had dug through to a promising layer of sandstone, and each morning when he surveyed the site it seemed he had made more progress than he thought. The weather had turned to a biting chill, and the hours of sunlight dwindled even further in the dim shadow cast by the encircling trees.

He returned one night to his room feeling especially pleased with himself, until he felt inside his tool bag and realised that it felt particularly light. His tools were not inside. George pushed down a rising sense of panic and glanced outside. His gaze was met with darkness. The moon was obscured by a thick curtain of cloud. Reluctantly, George resolved to retrace his steps.

The flickering beam from his lantern fell on nothing save dead leaves and brittle sticks. George was panting by the time he came upon the dig site. His eyes were surely playing tricks on him, for he spied a glimmering yellow light ahead. He stopped to catch his breath, and in between his ragged inhalations he heard the unmistakable sound of a shovel grinding against dirt. Exhaustion gave way to a hot rage.

Somebody was digging in his hole.

He crept forward. Quietly, haltingly. He reached the edge of the grove, and through the gloom he saw a cloaked figure perched on the lip of the hole. George made an incomprehensible noise and rushed forward to confront the mystery digger. The digger, surprised, attempted to turn towards George. There was a slip. A sudden fall. The black pit swallowed up the digger.

George leaned over the side with his lantern to illuminate the depths. The young woman, original finder of the tooth, lay at a crooked angle at the bottom of the hole. A dark stain pooled under her chin.

If he were a better man, one with less drive for self-preservation and more compassion for his fellow creatures, he might have leapt in after her to check her injuries. The shock of the body sprawled against the mud drove George to put as much space between the sight as possible. He was sweating profusely in his room before he had time to contemplate his best course of action.

Well, he decided, there would be nothing further to do until the morning. He would think more clearly after a good night of rest.

A nervous excitement kept him from falling into a deep sleep. He was awoken a short while after setting his head against the pillow by a soft noise at the door. Immediately, George sat up to survey the room. Nothing seemed amiss. His eyes glanced once again at the door. A tall shadow blocked the door frame. A scrunch of his eyes affirmed that the shadow was not actually a shadow, and was, in fact, the silhouette of a figure wearing a billowing cloak. George closed his eyes tightly.

When he looked again, the figure had stepped towards his bed. Slowly, the hood was removed to reveal the plump face of the young woman. Indignantly, George began to reprimand her for entering his chamber, but was interrupted by a hoarse croak escaping her opened mouth. Her jaw swung wide with a resonating crack, and her fleshy tongue pushed out a trove of stained, flat teeth which poured gracelessly to the floor. A great heave from the pit of her belly brought forth a wet trail of soil and sand, mixed heartily with what appeared to be a thick, green bile. A fetid smell forced George to lean helplessly over the side of the bed to expel the remains of his last meal.

When he had recovered, the woman was gone. The pulpy dirt mess was gone. The teeth remained, littered across the floor like strewn petals.

George was not superstitious. He considered himself to be an educated man, and prided himself on his ability to recognise that the apparition must have been caused by a manifestation of a guilty conscience following his rash departure from the dig site. He hurriedly pulled on his boots and overcoat, and was walking the trail before the realisation struck him that his mind could not possibly have manifested teeth into a physical state. He thrust that worry to the back of his thoughts and concentrated on the path.

Back at the dig site, George carefully placed the lantern at the edge of the hole, before clambering down the side. He felt his way around the bottom, frantically patting from one end to the other. There was no body. The woman was gone.

He almost laughed with relief. He stuck his fingers into the soil to pull himself out and reached upwards to the edge. A cold hand clasped around his fingers. The woman leaned down into the hole, her mouth hanging loose. A shower of pebbles sprayed from her lips and coated George's hair in shingle. He tried to pull his hand from her grip, but she held firm. George was trapped. Soil and spit filled the pit to the brim.

All that remained—stuck upright from the earth as sturdy as tiny gravestones—were four pale fingertips.

ELECIA PAGE writes spooky tales and ghost stories. She is the Assistant Director of Out for Blood, *a queer horror film festival based in Cambridgeshire, UK. Elecia enjoys reading gothic novels and roller skating (although not at the same time). She lives in the fens with her partner and a cat named Kimba.*

You can find Out for Blood *at @outforbloodfilmfest on Instagram.*

THE HUNGER

Sanaya Deas

Matt hadn't spoken to his family in three months before the letter came.

It was nothing but a worn-down piece of paper with the words *I Need You* scrawled across it. It was certainly his mother's small handwriting, but it was rushed and crooked, like her hands couldn't stop shaking when she wrote it.

There was also a small red stain in the corner, and it was unlike anything he'd ever seen. It was dry but sticky, and a harrowing shade of red. Seeing it, Matt couldn't think of anything other than blood.

Matt drove to Color Hills that night. The place looked just as Matt had left it—the wild forest that bordered town on all sides, the gas station across the street from the welcome sign, the post office in the town's center. The streets were empty, save for a couple wandering aimlessly down the main street. Matt called out to them, prepared to ask for directions.

The couple turned around slowly at the sound of his voice, and Matt's question died at his lips at the sight of them. Their faces were pale and sunken in, dry and wrinkly. They both offered up a smile, and it sent a shiver down Matt's spine so cold he turned the car's air conditioner off.

"Hello dear stranger!" greeted the man. His teeth were yellow, and red at the edges. "Are you hungry?"

"Uh—no, thank you. I'm just looking for Alice Goodman. I'm her son and I'm not quite sure where she lives now. Could you... help me out?"

The woman was happy to guide him. Her voice was just as sweet as her partner's and her smile just as wide. Her teeth, however, were redder.

Matt's fingers fumbled for the window controls as he thanked her for the directions.

"You sure you're not hungry?" she asked, "We've got some berries here if you'd like some!"

The window rolled shut, and Matt sped away.

Alice greeted her son at the doorway in a sing-song voice, "Oh sweetheart! I'm so glad to see you!" She held out cupped hands, and in them sat a bunch of red berries.

This couldn't have been his mother, Matt thought. She was more skeleton than human. The clothes she wore hung off her weak frame like curtains. She was nothing but her hollow face and wide eyes and pale skin.

Pale hands, stained red.

Matt took a long, slow breath and tried to steady his voice. "Glad to see you too, Ma. You okay? How's Maeve?" He stepped forward, reached out to touch her, but his mother flinched.

"Well, I'm just peachy now, seeing your face! Maeve's upstairs, but she's feeling a bit… unwell right now." Her smile widened. Teeth red to match her hands. "I saved these just for you! Won't you take a few?" she asked, lifting her outstretched hands higher.

"No thanks," Matt said, harsher than he'd meant to.

Alice's smile faltered.

"Not now, I mean," Matt quickly added, "It was a long drive from Cambridge. I'd just like to —rest—for a bit if that's okay?"

Alice's eyes were almost unrecognizable, but there was something behind those hazel orbs, something that was impossible for Matt to miss. The smile returned, and the skin around her mouth stretched.

"Of course!" She finally stepped aside. "They go great with dinner, you know!"

Maeve was feeling more than a bit unwell.

His sister, ten years old now, was a parting gift from his father, a miserable old bastard named Richard who died in a one-way crash on I-90. Maybe an accident. Maybe suicide. None of them knew, but now Matt supposed it didn't matter.

To end like that, a fiery explosion, or like this, withering away like a flower.

"Matty?" she whispered, as Matt opened the door. It took a considerable amount of effort to stop himself from throwing up. She looked like their mother—impossibly frail, except there was almost nothing behind her eyes. Maeve smiled, and it was nothing like the ones he'd seen before. It was more of a wince, small and crooked.

"Yeah, it's me," Matt wanted to say, but the words didn't come out. His voice cracked on the first syllable, and then he began to sob.

She was so small already. Not even a hundred pounds soaking wet. And yet the memories came rushing back—her running around on the playground, playing soccer with her friends, wrestling with one another when she was eight and he was fifteen and they both knew better but their mother never seemed to mind. And now she was nothing. Skin and bone.

There they were. Matt crying, Maeve watching. She watched his shoulders heave and his head shake. After an eternity he fell silent, and between them there was nothing but labored breaths and the whir of a fan in the background.

Maeve spoke. It was so low Matt almost missed it. "I'm okay Matty. Just hungry."

Matt watched wordlessly from the dinner table as his mother dumped nothing but those red berries into her blender. In turn, Alice stood unmoving as she studied the machine working. As soon as the blender went silent, she poured the soupy red substance into a dingy beige bowl and joined Matt at the table.

Alice swallowed a spoonful of the substance as if her life depended on it.

"Did you eat on the way here?" she asked pleasantly. "I bet you're starving. Would you like some?"

Matt's throat went dry. "No thanks. I'm not hungry."

Alice slammed her spoon onto the table and leapt forward. "Like *hell* you aren't!"

Matt forgot how to breathe. The fire in her eyes was hot, the knives in her voice sharp. They stared at each other for a long moment. Alice was so close to Matt's face he could smell the berries on her breath. The scent reminded Matt of cough medicine.

After an eternity, Alice cleared her throat and slowly sat back into her chair. "I'm sorry baby. I just—I don't want you getting sick like your sister. *She* didn't want to eat. Look at her now!"

The berries, six in the palm of his hand, were so light and delicate. The skin was peeling off one of them, exposing soft red underneath. Purple lines danced underneath it, almost like veins. Matt bagged them, carefully. Then, just as delicately, Matt came up to Maeve's room.

Her eyes were wide open, hazel orbs reflecting in the moonlight that seeped through the curtains.

"I don't close them, if I can help it," Maeve said, as Matt stepped forward. "Sometimes I—I get scared that I—won't be able to open them again."

Matt kneeled next to her bed and placed a gentle hand on hers. Her skin was cold and wrinkled. Her ten-year-old hands looked and felt like sixty.

"Maeve," he whispered, "I'm so sorry."

"You're leaving?"

Matt leaves, Maeve dies. This, he realized, was the cold hard truth.

"What'll happen to Mom?" Matt asked, and he kept his voice low to keep from sobbing again.

Maeve looked away from him then, studied the featureless white wall beside her. No posters, no family photos, no little trinkets. Had there ever been any? Or did she rip them off once their mother began to fade away, once she refused to eat? His sister let out a shaky breath.

"Nothing. It's...already happened."

"I don't understand."

"The berries—" Maeve's voice cracked. She tried to clear it, and the coughing was the worst sounding thing Matt'd ever heard. Each cough sounded like the most painful thing. "Once you get 'em... you won't need anything else. Won't—*want* anything else... either."

Maeve winced, and Matt realized his grip on her hand had tightened. He muttered an apology and placed his hands on his knees.

"You didn't eat them," he said.

"No." She locked eyes with Matt again. "I saw what it did... to the others. And once Mom got a hold of 'em—I knew it was over."

The weight of the berries in his pockets felt impossible. He should destroy them, squish them under his boots, but it would do no good. He needed to know what these things were.

"Why didn't you tell me?"

Maeve pondered his question for a moment. The silence left Matt to fill in the blanks himself. Because Mom wouldn't let her? Because she'd grown too weak? To protect him? Finally, she answered, "It doesn't matter now."

Matt closed his eyes for a long, hard moment. Then he stood to leave.

"Mom and I—" Matt froze. He didn't have the heart to turn around. The last image of his baby sister wouldn't be this.

And still, Maeve spoke. "We're both...the same. Both hungry."

Computer science major by day and author by night, SANAYA DEAS is a fan of messy characters, found families, and places that seem just a bit off. Two of her short stories have been published in Chroma, *Pace University's literary journal.*

FOR THE PLACE
WHERE MY BONES WILL LIE

Sam Lesek

It will be quiet there—

in the place where my bones

have been conquered by the seasons.

Time will pull the deep undergrowth

over me,

like a shroud,

and the snow will become my white sheet.

The birds will braid my hair

to keep their nests warm,

as the wasps and the flies sample

my leftovers.

And the animals,

with every mouthful,

between jagged canine teeth,

will take turns

ferrying me across

the River.

I, the bones,

will be a part of the landscape

as the landscape lays claim

to all the

parts of

me.

SAM LESEK is a writer of horror and dark fiction from Toronto, Canada. Her stories have been published by Scare Street, Black Hare Press, and Black Ink Fiction. Find her on Twitter @SamLesek.

THE DEVOUR OF THE SADDLE FLOWER

Sara Crocoll Smith

The front door slammed behind Erica as she raced to tie her gym shoes. She heard her kids screaming—*mommy, mommy, mommy*—from within the tiny two-story home.

Gray clouds gathered. She hoped the rain might be good for her neglected flowerbeds, a brown, sad welcome to the Turner household. But she wasn't sure anything could breathe life back into them and return the garden to its previous glory.

The soles of her shoes pounded the pavement while her husband's words echoed in her head.

"You said that last time. But Bella is almost two now and you're not getting any younger." Fresh from work in his button-down shirt and slacks, Steve touched her lower back.

Erica snorted, pulled away. She turned off the pasta before the water boiled over. Legos crashed behind her, and Aiden wailed. "Marissa, will you cut that out! Leave your brother alone." Erica spun her daughter toward the dining room. "Help get the table ready, please."

Erica crouched, comforting her son briefly. She cursed on her way to the cupboard, cringing from the sharp pain of stepping on a stray Lego, then readied their plates for dinner.

Steve's voice softened. He wrapped his arms around her so sweetly that she didn't resist his embrace this time. Yet her chest tightened, and her breath came quick and shallow. "You know what I mean. We should try for the fourth soon."

His hand traveled to her stomach, caressing in circles. Oppressive heat floated from the stovetop. Erica's forehead beaded with sweat. Silverware clattered in the other room. More crying. She squirmed.

"Dinner's getting cold."

Steve leaned against the counter, folded his arms. "Is this about your claustrophobia? I don't understand how pregnancy triggers—"

Erica's nostrils flared. She took a big breath, trying to drown out the noise and concentrate. "Can you *please* get the kids seated? We can talk about this later."

He rolled his eyes at her, waving a hand dismissively. "Come on, kids."

Erica bit her lip as the children calmed the moment Steve entered the dining room. She'd only just finished putting the food on the table and sat down when the dog barked. Erica glanced at her husband, downing his dinner and oblivious to the hungry dog.

She sighed, got up, and fed the dog too.

Before she could sit back down, Steve looked up. "Could you get me a glass of water, honey?"

Erica gritted her teeth and returned to the kitchen. Holding the glass under the faucet, she stared as the water burbled up, overflowing into the sink basin.

"Honey? The water?"

"Mom!"

"Mommy!"

Her grip on the glass tightened until she thought she might break it. She squeezed her eyes shut, then opened them and delivered the water to Steve. Her feet carried her toward the door before she knew what was happening. "I'm going for a jog. Be back in half an hour."

"What? But how do I—"

Like pushing through a viscous membrane, Erica crossed the threshold and stole away from the house. Her rhythmic pace as she jogged along the road and onto the trail comforted her. The darkening clouds warned her to be out of the woods and back home in time.

Guilt tugged at her. Yet the further she went, the better she felt amongst the sprawling greenery. She could *breathe*. It brought back mornings she'd spent in her own garden, before their first baby girl, surrounded by burgeoning flora she'd nurtured.

Erica ran deeper along the trail, past hemlocks, past maidenhair ferns, past saddle flowers—past the point at which she knew she should turn back. Her muscles burned and still she went farther, faster.

The trail curved ahead. She sprinted, ignoring the stinging in her lungs. Reaching the bend, she scooted to a stop, doubled over, and kneaded the stitch in her side. Her shoe had come untied, so she stooped to fix it. Her nose runny from the exertion, Erica sniffed—a pungent musk wafted from nearby.

She straightened and found herself face to face with a stately buck. Rays of sunshine, a rare break of the sunset through the storm clouds, splayed around its meaty shoulders and thick torso. The animal lifted its head high, towering over her. Its antlers sprouted like a magnificent crown from its skull.

Frozen, her eyes widened when the buck lowered its muzzle, clawed the ground with its hoof. She flinched when it chuffed, its breath steamy.

The buck charged at her.

Erica barreled in the opposite direction, not caring she'd veered off the trail. Her singular focus was flight—dodging tree trunks, leaping over roots, ducking branches. Sweat rained down her back and her cheeks grew hot, but she didn't stop. Another chuff behind her, so close she imagined she felt the buck's warm breath on her neck. Erica sped up, screaming when her shoelace caught—

—and she fell, tumbling into darkness.

She landed in water, submerged until she found unsteady footing on a soft surface and erupted into the air, sputtering. Plunged into chest-heigh water, Erica gazed up. Her eyes stung and her skin tingled, but she didn't think she'd broken any bones.

Veined purple walls encircled her. Fifteen feet above, a tubular opening highlighted the silhouette of the buck peering down at her.

"Help!" she screamed.

The buck disappeared. She continued yelling as she pressed her hands along the walls of her prison, strangely familiar in a way she couldn't quite place. They were too high to climb, and any progress she made attempting to escape was thwarted by thick, prickly hairs pointed downward.

Erica moved to the center. "Help! Anyone?"

She'd passed no one on the trail out here—she'd been the only one crazy enough to venture out in the coming storm. A fat raindrop landed square on her nose. Another on her cheek. Another. Soon, the rain came down in sheets.

Shivering, she hugged herself and rubbed her upper arms. A sweetness lingered on her tongue. She dipped her fingers in the water and tasted—nectar? Again, she returned to the wall, purple with squiggly veins that showed in relief every time lightning brightened the sky. Covering her mouth, she stepped back. It couldn't be. It wasn't possible.

A staple in her garden once upon a time, pitcher plants, which she preferred to call by their lesser-known name saddle flower, were carnivorous. Prey, like salamanders, would fall into the open-mouthed pitcher and—

"Drown," she whispered.

Relentless, the rain beat upon her, splashing the surface of the water. Her breathing intensified until she stumbled from dizziness. The water was now at her shoulders and showing no signs of stopping.

Her skin burned. Erica touched her clothes, only to find them patchy and disintegrating. Her mouth formed a small 'o'—pitcher plants slowly digested their prey. The water tickled her neck. She longed to be home, safe and dry. She'd never envisioned dying, not at her age, not like this.

Erica took a deep breath and closed her eyes. The chaos of her life subsided. The whining, the crying, the needing, the demanding—it receded. Buoyed was the intoxicating smell of her children's heads, a soft kiss from her husband before her eyes opened in the morning, the giggles and the cuddles, the love and the fullness.

From the marrow of her soul, she called upon everything her life was, the good and the bad, and launched herself upward. Vaulting out of the water, she grabbed the lip of the pitcher plant.

Only the tips of her fingers curled over the edge. Slick from rain, she could gain no ground. Inch by inch, she lost the battle until, finally, she slipped.

Underneath the water, Erica thrashed. The surface eluded her. Her arms lashed out, to fight, to hit, to do anything. Her hand bumped into something hard, and she gripped it. She ran her fingers over the object—one end was bulbous, the other sharp. Feeling for the plant wall, Erica jabbed the sharp end at the leaf and sliced it open.

Spilling forth in a great wave, she landed on the forest floor. Her naked skin raw, she stared at the saddle flower, split open like a womb. When she looked down at her instrument of freedom, she saw she held a broken femur bone. Tears threatened at the corners of her eyes, but never quite came. At last, she rose to her feet, returned to the trail. The storm abated, washing her clean of the plant's digestive acid as she walked steadily home.

Erica traversed the path up her front walk, ignoring the forlorn flowerbeds. Her garden wouldn't remain untended any longer. Yet she didn't plan to do it alone. She'd teach Bella, Aiden, and Marissa, among other things, how to care for a saddle flower. Standing in front of the door to her household, not a stitch of clothes on her, she lifted her chin and straightened her shoulders.

Erica knocked on the door.

SARA CROCOLL SMITH is the author of the ghostly gothic horror series Hopeful Horror. *She's also the publisher and editor-in-chief of* Love Letters to Poe, *a haven to celebrate the works of Edgar Allan Poe. For an exclusive morsel of gothic ghosts and daylight horror, visit SaraCrocollSmith.com/Ivy to get the free short story "The Strangle of Ivy".*

CARE INSTRUCTIONS

Ian A. Bain

Congratulations on the purchase of your new plant baby! You are joining millions around the globe in finding homes for the thought-to-be-extinct *Morte Fatum*, commonly known as the Purple Pod™.

You've probably already noticed that your Pod is not in bloom upon delivery. If you follow the instructions below, you should have your Purple Pod™ blooming in no time!

1. Our custom-built transport vans should have kept your plant hydrated and healthy. Immediately upon delivery, set your thermostat to 80^0F/29^0C. Ensure your humidity is between 82-85% using a combination of humidifiers and dehumidifiers.

2. If you come home from work and the plant has wilted, it's because it missed you. Take tomorrow off from work and spend the day with your Purple Pod™. You will find a stack of doctor's notes in your care package to be given to your employer.

3. If black ooze drips from the Pod, your plant is angry with you. Here are our top tips for soothing your Purple Pod™ :

1) Review steps 1 and 2.

2) If you have been giving more attention to your plants, spouse, or children, you will need to stop this immediately! The Pod gets jealous easily. Try bringing the Pod with you as you run errands, or take the Pod into bed with you at night. If you have a spouse, ask them to spend the night on the couch. If they're truly a partner, they'll understand.

3) Purple Pods™ love music. To increase your bond, the music should come from your own voice. If you sing to the point of your throat drying, tearing, and bleeding, spit some of that blood into the Pod's soil to show them how much you care.

   You should probably take tomorrow off from work. Use another doctor's note, found in your care package.

4. To get your Purple Pod™ to bloom:

   1) Ensure you have followed all previous steps.

   2) Purple Pods™ require serious time, energy, and sacrifice. If you have managed to maintain your job up to this step, it is time to quit, and devote your life to the Pod. A resignation letter can be found in your care package.

   3) Because you spat your esophageal blood into the soil in step 3, your Purple Pod™ now has a taste for blood sacrifice. Animal blood should suffice, for a time. You can start with roadkill, or baby birds fallen from nests,

but eventually, the Purple Pod™ will want more. It will require something you love.

Spend some time loving your sacrifice and do it in front of your Pod. After a week or so, hang your pet/child/spouse above the Pod and drain them like a cow.

4) Do not be alarmed by the vines that are now surely growing from your Purple Pod™. The Pod is using its feelers to keep track of you at all times, no matter where you are in your house. Your Pod loves you.

5) Eventually, your Pod will become bored of these sacrifices. You will know your Pod wants more by looking directly into the purple flowers growing from its feelers. If you see the faces of those you've sacrificed in the centre of these flowers, your Pod is ready for greater sacrifice.

6) In your care package, find the "Blood-Letting" kit. Follow the attached instructions. Be sure to have sugar cookies nearby.

5. If you have followed the above instructions perfectly, your Purple Pod™ is now ready to bloom! Stay with your Pod until the next full moon. If the next full moon is far away, do not be alarmed if your Pod's feelers insert themselves into your blood-letting wounds. Your Pod's just hungry!

6. The majesty of *Morte Fatum* in bloom cannot be captured by the English language. Once your Pod has bloomed, look

directly into the main flower to experience the full breadth of wonder. Let the multi-dimensional hellscape within wash over and consume you. Do not resist the vines that grab you. Soon, the Pod's visions will unravel you; will unravel the Universe. Do not despair, rejoice! For every soul devoured, your Pod will propagate ten-fold. Welcome, Devourer of Worlds!

For customer service and troubleshooting, call 1-888-555-6666. No Refunds.

IAN A. BAIN (he/him) is a writer of dark fiction living in Muskoka, Ontario. Ian's work has recently appeared in Not Deer Magazine *and* The Crypt Online Magazine. *Ian can be stalked online at @bainwrites on Twitter.*

REAP AND SOW

Ashley Van Elswyk

Farm we call her, this ancient being
who shudders beneath us with a scoff. She, who is
the murmur of worms wrung through soil,
the peony bloom, the fruit dripping nectar,
stones clacking under a thunderstorm's fists,
roots groaning with the strain of spread.
She turns her gaze toward us,
our knees licked with dust, our nails stealing silt,
and wonders how we'll taste.
Swallowing slag, poison, spilt seeds, we sow
infection—but she is patient, knows slow growth
will yield a sweeter crop to glut herself upon.
Our plows hack the lines of her face, carve out
eternity, less scarred than remade. She slouches
over the rock beds, splits then draws them up—
and granite-toothed she grins and spits
these boulders at our feet, a proud predator

whose trophies break the blades that sliced her smile.

She parches herself to a desert, picks her teeth with

brittle stalks; then gathers pools to drown herself in rot.

Chewing slowly, crop after crop returns to her gut.

Her wraiths come clothed in dun and grey, claws

sinking into the slick of her rain-drunk surface,

following the paths of her veins to our home

to fill our sleep with wailing shadows, hungry maws.

In the daylight hours, her scavengers swoop

down to bury their beaks deep into our hoard,

gutting pepper flesh, plucking seeds as easily as eyes.

Give and take, and give and take and take.

The harvesters curse. The harvesters, desperate, disperse.

She returns the peas when we plant our teeth,

the currants swell with blood,

for carrots, our fingers, and squash our sinew,

we lose our skulls to the cauliflower fields,

peel skin for onions, rip hair out for leeks,

ball our tongues into tomatoes, our flesh into beets,

and the *farm* she laughs and eats and eats,

gorging on our sweat and tears and pleas

until we've poured all of ourselves into her—

buried in her belly under the dirt.

Farm we called her, and she did not fight

at first—this land is a subtler beast,

her body bears life, but she lives on the dead,

made from the decomposed and decaying

and us, her self-proclaimed keepers, we join

the bone dust and shells and long-digested flesh.

Ghosts of her children lie blooming in stone

and deeper still, remnants of a primordial ocean

ebb and flow in the sand of her skin.

We sow and we reap, and are reaped and are sown.

ASHLEY VAN ELSWYK is a queer Canadian writer of speculative fiction and poetry, who finds inspiration in art, and getting lost in nature. Her work appears in Green Ink Poetry, From the Farther Trees, Idle Ink, *and the* Hundred Word Horror: Home *and* Dark Hearts *anthologies. She can be found on twitter at @ashvanewrites.*

CORNER LOT

Armand Rosamilia

You wouldn't know to look at the overgrown corner lot, but there's a house there. Behind the tulip trees, silver bells, black spruces and red oaks, shielded by the bearberries, mountain laurels and northern bayberry, covered by pretty black-eyed Susans and trumpet honeysuckle, a two-story wood-and-concrete structure stands.

I've lived at 251 Center Avenue since the day I was born. Fifty years. Just me and momma. After the day I was brought home from the hospital (I was born in nearby Red Bank), I never left. Homeschooled from the beginning. My momma had what would now be diagnosed as schizophrenia. A touch of bipolar and paranoia, too. All undiagnosed, because we never left the property.

Would you believe, before I stepped onto the overgrown lot across the street, I'd never even ventured onto the asphalt of Center Avenue itself? You might be thinking: this poor, poor woman. Never saw the world. Never got to meet anyone or do anything with her life.

I would wholeheartedly disagree. See, I got a better education than the public-school kids. I got one-on-one teaching, and then when the computer age came along, it opened up a world to explore. Maybe I didn't travel to Italy or New York City physically, but I was there. I read everything I could get my hands on. Momma ordered crates of used books for me. I walked the streets of Chicago using Google Earth. I devoured documentaries on Netflix and listened to history and true crime podcasts.

I was never interested in fiction. I wanted to explore the real world. Things that were explainable. Things that happened.

Which is why the overgrown lot across the street was a puzzle.

In 1974, I believe it was either June or July, I do remember it was warm, even for summer, the first boy went missing. I've gone back through the online archives of the *Asbury Park Press* as well as the *Newark Times*. No mention is made before that summer.

The house had been exquisite in her heyday. Back when the rich from Manhattan drove down in their fancy cars for a quiet shore getaway. It was owned by a Hungarian family. Momma said they were prone to loud violence, and you always knew when they were down for a week or two. They'd throw wild parties. Drink alcohol. Dance to loud music.

By the time I was old enough to understand, the parties had stopped. The house was quiet. Every now and then, I'd spy a light on in the home. A shadow moving around. A car or two in the driveway, but nothing out of the ordinary.

That came later.

When I was twelve, in 1983, the vehicles stopped coming. Our little seaside town was no longer a getaway spot for the New York elite. I had no idea back then, because there was no computer or Google Earth to allow me to walk the streets, but our seaside hamlet was shrinking. Fading away, one lot at a time. Near the bay, several homes had been destroyed by a Nor'easter. Another half dozen by the bulldozer, to clear the area for condominiums that would never rise over the water.

The house across the street, on the corner lot, was silent. The grass had begun to grow higher, a foot tall in places. The weeds began their choking march across the property, too. Later I'd learn the original family had died out and another family, these people also Hungarian, had purchased it. Perhaps with the intent of rebuilding or tearing it down. The lot was nearly a square acre, a throwback to when the houses in our town weren't built on top of one another, parcels cut into fourths and sold.

I spent my teen years in my own tiny world, learning. Staying busy. Content. By then, momma had inherited her parent's estate. She'd also been receiving child support for me from my absent father. I knew I could easily find him online, but the thought of it made me sad. What if he had a new, better daughter he doted on? Took her to Keansburg amusement park. Great Adventure. A trip to Disney in Florida. I couldn't stand the thought of being robbed of these actual trips, so I pushed it aside.

Butterfly weed was the first perennial I identified across the street, and it hosted such beautiful monarch caterpillars (and later, of course, butterflies) that it brought me to tears. I've never cried so much. Even when momma passed, I shed tears, but nothing as emotional.

It was also the same week another little boy went missing. I remember the police searched the property, but by then the weeds had overtaken the grass. Almost overnight, the mix of trees had begun to grow as well. A wall of shrubbery, long rows of flowers, and a seemingly impenetrable wall of thorns had sprung up, blocking the property from a casual onlooker.

I never dated a boy or (later) a man. Yes, I had plenty of online suitors. I even toyed with one of those dating apps where you swipe left. Or was it right? But the thought of having someone on my block, in my home, touching me… no thank you.

Studies took up most of my adult life. I loved biology. I took online courses from several colleges about autopsies, taxidermy, botany, and the like. I wanted to know how the human body worked, what made us tick. I wanted to know about the plant life growing so wildly across the street. Why had someone never complained about the lot? Reading through local news feeds and message boards, this town was filled with busybodies who pointed out every little thing their neighbors did.

A fourth boy went missing. Then another two, all the year before my momma died. By then, momma was frail. She rarely ventured to the front porch to crochet or stare across the street.

It'll be gone soon. The house. The signs of mankind. The bodies, she'd say. *Given back to the earth, where it all belongs.*

At the time I didn't understand her. Now I most surely do.

When she died, peacefully in her sleep, I didn't bother calling the authorities. They wouldn't know what her last wish was, but I did.

The house and the bank accounts were all in my name. I made sure we were fed, with weekly food deliveries from A&P. Pizza on Friday night, the driver leaving the box on the tray near the door, where he'd find his generous tip.

Momma died on a Friday night. She wasn't feeling well so I ate her half of her pepperoni and onion pizza, too. We never ate leftovers. Besides, Saturday was always ham and cheese sandwiches for lunch and meatloaf for dinner.

I took her across the street two minutes to midnight on Saturday, right after I'd gotten everything in order: her clothes, her books, her personal items. I'd been the cook for us for years. I cleaned the dishes. Made sure I had all the ingredients for pasta on Sunday.

I'd need to cut the food in half now that she was gone.

Momma wasn't heavy in my arms. I walked onto the pavement, and it was an odd feeling. Across to the corner lot, where the pin oaks parted, careful not to drop their acorns on us. The northern spicebush pulled back, clearing my path to the house.

Inside I went, as if I'd been here before. Through the rooms and into the basement, the door long gone.

Momma had told me every step as I got older. The tasks that needed to be done.

I would take over her guardianship of the corner lot. Keep it free of invading children, who'd grow up and graffiti the walls. Leave empty beer cans and cigarette butts.

There was a shovel in the corner, and a crudely drawn map of the burial locations. Momma had already marked where she wanted to be, in the direct center of the basement. Overlooking her work.

Overlooking my new work, yet to come.

ARMAND ROSAMILIA is a New Jersey boy currently living in sunny Florida, writing horror and crime thrillers full-time and truly living the dream. He has over 200 releases to date in his thirty years of publishing stories, and he hopes to keep it going as long as he can. He also loves coffee, M&Ms, bourbon and Funko Pops. Find out more at https://armandrosamilia.com.

THE HEARTWOOD

Sally Hughes

As soon as my mother felt labour come on and knew she could not be quiet, she ran out of the house and into the woods. When she reached the tree, she crawled backwards, on all fours like an animal, into the deep crack on the trunk's side. Only once her heaving belly was hidden in the dark hollow did she cry her pain aloud.

My mother told me this as we walked hand in hand to the ribbon of woodland that clung to the hillside, bordered by the motorway above and the railway below. She told me how the tree had trembled with each spasm, and rocked its leaves in sympathy with her agony. She traced her bruised fingers across the pitted bark, and told me how I finally surged from her body and landed in the soft mulch at the tree's heart. I had not cried. Cradled in a second womb of wood, I had lain so quietly that she had been afraid to turn around and look at me.

Later, when I woke to find my father sleeping and my mother missing, I ran to the tree. I called for my mother over and over, but she did not answer. When I realised she was gone for good, I crawled into the hollow. The tree gathered itself around me, sighing faintly, as

I rubbed my damp face against the jagged heartwood. I felt it pierce my skin, draw my blood.

From that day, the tree held me as gently as it held the dusky moths, the fluttering pigeons, the fleshy ropes of ivy. I whispered my darkness into its bark, and felt it distilled into leaves of green and gold and red, into honey-thick sap.

As I grew, the tree carried every one of my secrets; a more-than-mother, a more-than-lover. The only peace I knew was within the circle cast by its huge canopy. After school I took library books and read them under the shelter of the branches until the light drained from the sky and the wood mice began their scratching. I left the books in the tree's wrinkles and scars until they bloomed vivid orange spots of mould. One midsummer, I scattered torn pages around its trunk as a kind of offering, and by winter they had dissolved and disappeared back into the earth.

When I went to university it was agonizing. I did not go far—only forty minutes away on the bone-rattling train—but it was enough for me to feel the pain of separation, like an axe thrust in my belly. Away from the woods, the humiliations and miseries swelled within me until my skin was taut. Every Friday afternoon, I took the train home, and when I saw the tree again, my secrets burst out of me. I spent my weekend nights curled within its heartwood, only sleeping when all the words had spilled from my mouth, and I felt my strength returning.

Then my father died, and the house was mine, and I knew I was finally safe and would never be parted from the tree again.

But then I met him.

It was a soft October afternoon. He had snuck away from the volunteers he was supposed to be managing to go foraging. The best mushrooms in the woods grew in a soft cloud above the tree's spreading roots. He cooked them for me over a fire with butter and fresh thyme, watched as I bit into the flesh and licked mushroom juice from my lips.

He said that I looked like a dryad and should be called Daphne. I told him he would never need to chase me, for his hair was the colour of split birch, his eyes the fresh green of spring beech leaves. When I undressed him, his long pale body opened up like the finely veined petals of an anemone.

I did not lie to him, but he did not understand me. He had read too many fairy tales, and expected me to be a Snow White, a Briar Rose, with a splinter of weakness at my heart that he would be the one to suck out.

At first, he took my lack of weakness as a lack of openness. Then, as time passed, he began to realise where my strength came from. And I was careless. One too many times, he caught me crouched down in front of the open washing machine, burying my face into his dirty clothes, drawing in the smell of the trees. One too many times, I pulled him to bed when he came in stinking of the underbrush.

Though I saw his jealousy, I was complacent. Such jealousy could not be acted upon, or even articulated. And it was helpless against the power of the tree, which had endured for an age, which would outlive us both.

I had underestimated him. Like a canker in his brain, the suspicion grew. I would never be a Red-Riding Hood, whimpering for a man with an axe. My story was an older one, a wilder one. I did not need a woodcutter. I needed the woods.

But without the tree, I would wither and weaken. Without the tree, I would become the dependent child he wanted me to be.

One fiery autumn afternoon he came back with a look of fearful triumph on his face and a trailer of split logs. He said the tree had been a danger; one bough had already snapped off in an autumn storm. Nursery children used the woods for forest school. It couldn't be risked any longer.

I did not stay to hear more. I ran to the woods, the shuddering breath catching in my chest.

He had delighted in his massacre. Remains were strewn carelessly across the ground; a torn limb here, a chunk of heartwood there. A jagged semi-circle was all that was left of the trunk. Unripe acorns were scattered amongst the wreckage like pale, milky jewels.

I collapsed into the dried leaf litter where I had been born. I dug my fingers into the earth and clawed downwards until I found something. Roots. Spreading, twisting roots. Roots that joined with other roots, in looping, swirling strands of life and death. Roots that did not end. Roots that had not died.

He had forgotten the roots.

I crouched down, put my face to the ground, and breathed in the living scent. Then I began to speak. I told the roots of my pain, my anger. I whispered my fury until it dripped from my chin, slithered through the lichen, and snaked down into the earth.

Deep underground, something stirred.

Above me, the ghost of leaves shivered.

When I knew I had been heard, I went back to the house, and put my head on his chest, as he had always wanted me to. He went to sleep happy. I lay awake, holding one acorn tight in my trembling fist.

The next day, I found a ring of mushrooms surrounding the tree's ruins. They were smooth and white as hard-boiled eggs, and I had to squint to see the fine dusting of grey that was all that showed what was within.

I cooked them for him with butter and fresh thyme, watched as he bit into their flesh and licked grey mushroom juice off his chin.

When it was over, and moss green bile bubbled from his gaping mouth, I took the acorn from my pocket. Warmed by my blood, it had turned a rich copper brown.

I walked to the woods.

SALLY HUGHES lives in the Scottish Highlands and works as a library supervisor. She has a PhD in literature, and is currently seeking representation for her first novel, a Gothic mystery set in 1860s Yorkshire. Her ghost story "Milk" is included in Blood & Bone: An Anthology of Body Horror by Women & Non-Binary Writers, *published by Ghost Orchid Press. She tweets at @sallyhbooks.*

NEON FLY

S.J. Townend

The swarm of fluorescent green flies hovers above Mother's head as she's taken for cremation by the army. Buckled over in pain, her guts are being digested from the inside out. A web of foamy green plaque coated in gelatinous, congealed blood spreads out from the rot that has perforated her bowels. A time ago, I would've shielded Eden's eyes from such a sight, but my child has seen it all before. We're all damaged goods, even those of us who are clean.

Through the transparent wall separating us, dry-eyed, Mother mouths the only words left that need to be said: "I love you. Look after Eden."

The cull has been going on for so long now, the nation's tears are spent.

The majority of the world chose to lead a lifestyle of poor-quality food choices, so, like the ocean and the soils, their bodies too are riddled with nano-plastics. Bacteria modified by scientists to break these plastics down proved successful to a degree in the oceans, but the same microbes are also drawn to the motes of plastic that saturate ninety-nine percent of the population's intestines. Oceans, lakes, rivers, have all become green, caked in thick sludge and stinking of rot and decay as all life within them perishes. Flies, neon lights in the night, swarm everywhere, hovering over the freshly deceased and the not so freshly deceased, feeding, laying eggs, spreading maggots. A stench worse than a butcher's neglected trashcan hangs everywhere, so much so that survivors have almost become immune to the petulant odour.

Of course, food chains developed: phosphorescent greenfly consume the plastic-gorging bacteria. Where one is found, the other follows.

"I love you," I shout from the other side of the Perspex screen. It stretches sky-high like the Babel Tower, but rather than separating people by race or language, it keeps those contaminated from the organic-fed.

"This way, madam." A guard hurries us into the tunnel toward the screening zone. I know we'll pass, myself and Eden. I've known since I was weaned that what we put into our mouth is what we become. I turned down platefuls of food as a child, knowing that my mother had been cutting corners, dishing up processed meats, offal, cheaply farmed nutrient-depleted vegetables. I turned it all down. She used to send me unfed to my room, cursing me for refusing to eat the meals she'd toiled arduously over. But I knew it was bad. All bad.

I raised Eden in a commune. We still visited Mother and stayed at her house, but we never ate her food. Our cooperative of like-minded farmers worked our patch of land organically. We ate sparsely, but we ate well. There were no shreds of plastic in our bodies; nothing for the bacteria and the flies that followed to feast upon. I was hopeful that some of the barefoot children Eden had grown up with, had pulled snails and slugs from the organic lettuces and radishes with, would be on board our ship too.

Before the bacteria started to digest us, before the neon fly came, the World Government's plans for shipping out the rich, the elite, the leaders and their families had been kept secret, but the truth eventually spilled. As the neon fly spread, leaders spoke out and confirmed the leaked escape conspiracy. Most of those that'd been on the list to be ejected from Earth in a light speed rocket had already perished. They'd been eaten from inside out, had fallen to the floor as a collection of green sludge and congealed blood, or had been found contaminated and pushed alive into funeral pyres which plumed yet more smoke into Earth's fucked atmosphere. The government had been terra-forming Mars for decades, and now that the leaders lacked numbers of the elite to seed Mars with, any civilians who passed the tests were to be given the chance to be shipped out, to colonize the red planet.

If civilians could prove they weren't contaminated, that they were clean of plastic, bacteria and neon fly, then they, too, could qualify for one of the twenty-three rockets launching this week.

"Mummy, I'm hungry." Eden squeezes my hand. She didn't even shed a tear when her grandmother was led away for combustion. "Can I get something out of the bag?"

"Not now, Eden." I'm pulling my entire belongings along behind us in a wheeled flight case. Eden is pulling hers. "There's food onboard. We just need to get through the checks."

"Okay."

I pick up the pace. The remnants of the World Government say there are enough spaces for all the uncontaminated, but I don't believe a word. I want to make sure we get on that ship. Barging past the other civilians, I can see the first checkpoint. There, we'll be examined medically for any signs of the green plaque. At the second point, our IQ will be tested. The new Solar Government state that there will be academic limits placed on those seeding the red planet. I've forewarned Eden of this, told her to dumb things down a little, but I can tell she's fearful of lying, because when she's nervous, she gets hungry.

We smash the physical and head towards the second checkpoint, but the crowd thickens as we approach it. I lose Eden for about ten minutes. This time feels like hours and I break into a sweat, pushing through the throngs of hopefuls, searching for my six-year-old. I find her sitting against a wall. Her bag is open, its contents are poking out, a multitude of colours, like the green and red guts which splayed from Father when we found him in the yard and were left no choice but to call Pest Control to have him exterminated.

"Thank God, Eden. I thought I'd lost you," I say, and grab and squeeze my child. She's all that I have left in this world and the next.

She smells so sweet. The softness of her hair comforts me, but she pulls away with a look of guilt on her face.

"What's wrong?"

"Nothing, Mummy. I thought... I thought I'd lost you. I was so hungry and scared—"

"Hold my hand," I say. "We just need to clear the second gate and then we're through to Solar System passport control."

I reach and pat our passport cards which are safely in my inner pocket, a lifetime's worth of paperwork compressed into memory chips that will allow us to embark on new lives, up on that small red dot which is nearly invisible from Earth—not because it's daytime, but because clouds of green-grey pollution have made a hazy, indecipherable mess of the sky.

We make it through the final gates, through the airlock and onto the ship. I smile with just my mouth at Eden. "We've made it," I say. She can sense trepidation in my words.

An official directs one hundred or so of us through to the seated area where we belt up for take-off. Eden nabs a window seat. I tell her to wave goodbye to Earth as we rise up, into, and through the clouds, as we break the ionosphere, leaving the pull of our wasted planet's gravity behind.

"Goodbye, Earth," she says, and I reach over to wave off, too, the concrete launch pad, which becomes a curve of grey, which becomes a ball of sludge-green encapsulated by a fuzzy neon halo, which becomes a ruined dot encased in green plaque. The once-blue oceans found in picture books of our planet are no longer present.

A light flashes above our heads, instructing us we're free to unbuckle, to move around the ship.

"Shall we find the food hall?" I say, trying to find positives in the journey lying ahead of us.

"I'm not hungry," she says.

"You were starving earlier," I say. Her eyes avoid mine. I notice a sprinkling of crumbs decorating the corners of her mouth. "What have you eaten?" I'm whispering, yet the air blows from my lips like rocket-plume.

"Sorry, Mummy." Tears collect in the corners of her eyes. "Earlier, when I lost you, I opened the packet of biscuits that Grandma gave me last year. I packed them as a memory of her, even though you told me never to eat them. I was so scared—so scared and so hungry."

A pulse of vomit rises up into my throat. I don't recall ever allowing Mother to ply my child with junk. How dare she. I curse Mother aloud as more tears fall down Eden's cheek. Through the window, I see a red ball in the distance growing larger. Our new home is under an hour away. I wipe the crumbs from my daughter's lips and pull her in tight to my chest.

"It's okay. I'm sorry for being angry with you."

It's at this point I notice a red neon fly hovering by my daughter's ear. And another. And another.

SJ TOWNEND has been creatively tapping at her keyboard for a few years after being advised to 'try writing' as therapy for post-natal depression. She has destroyed two laptops in that time but has discovered that the more she types, the less she cries.

Currently seeking representation for her first collection of short horror stories (working title: Sick Girl Writes*), SJ has also self-published two dark mystery novels centred loosely around the underground Bristol rave scene (both available on Amazon:* Tabitha Fox Never Knocks, Twenty-Seven & the Unkindness of Crows*).*

SJ is volunteer EIC for UK-based writing charity GLITTERY LITERARY. GL provides a platform for budding authors whilst raising money for children living in poverty: @GlittLit www.glitteryliterary.com

Lurking on Twitter: @SJTownend

HIGHLAND HOLIDAY

Birgit K. Gaiser

Kayleigh led the way down the Devil's Staircase. Her freckled face beamed as she surveyed the Highland landscape. She stopped to let Mike and Damian catch up, then pointed out the peaks of the Three Sisters in the distance. Even with the sky packed with low, grey clouds, Glencoe was breathtakingly beautiful. Its ancient, grey volcanic rock contrasted perfectly with the green of woodlands and heath below.

"Glad you came?" she asked.

"I guess it's slightly more picturesque than London," Damian quipped.

Mike simply stood with his mouth open as his head swivelled from left to right. "Whoa! This is amazing!"

They continued their descent down the path. The humidity increased noticeably, and low pressure threatened rain. Sweat, unable to evaporate in the oppressive air, trickled down their necks and faces, and they swatted at clouds of bloodthirsty midges. Despite the flatter terrain, the hike felt more challenging than it had in the mountains.

When they finally arrived at their destination, they were in dire need of a shower, dinner, and a pint. They settled into a booth, waiting for their fish and chips, when Kayleigh heard the dreaded question.

"Is there a doctor here?"

She waited a few seconds, then sighed, rolled her eyes at her companions, and got up. So much for being on holiday.

"I'm a general practitioner. What's the problem?"

"My girlfriend has a bad rash," a brunette woman said, in a soft Scandinavian accent.

Kayleigh sat down at their table and gestured at the nosy onlookers to mind their own business.

"Look," the second woman said, holding out her arms.

Kayleigh saw a handful of red spots that looked like insect bites. They were surrounded by dry, scaly skin in thin, red rings, reminiscent of the fungal ringworm infections she knew from her practice, but angrier, more clearly defined. Red scratch marks showed all over her arms, some of them bloody.

"Have you been scratching?" Kayleigh asked.

"I can't stop," the woman said, beginning to sob. "I even scratch in my sleep. It's driving me mad, insane!"

Kayleigh was aghast. The woman was far more distressed than the rash warranted.

"I can't help you much right now," she said, "but you should go to the nearest town and find a pharmacy. It's likely fungal, your bites probably got infected somehow. In the meantime, use fresh towels every day and keep your skin dry."

Kayleigh left them discussing next steps and returned to her group and her dinner.

Hikers, mountain bikers, and climbers filled the breakfast bar, stocking up on deep-fried calories before another day of exercise. The TV on the wall showed a BBC Scotland feature on unprecedented numbers of midges in the Highlands, exacerbated by the warm and humid spring.

"That's climate change for you," Damian sighed, shaking his head. "Better double up on the insect repellent."

The news was perfectly timed: they were going to hike through prime midge territory today, across Rannoch Moor, a desolate landscape of bogs, lakes, and yellowish grass.

The air was still oppressive, and the grey sky made the bleak landscape even less inviting. Midges were indeed present in high numbers and hung in clouds over the moor's standing water. Attracted by carbon dioxide and body heat, they swarmed any hikers they encountered with a hungry buzz.

"The BBC weren't kidding about the little bastards," Mike muttered. "No wonder the Romans built Hadrian's Wall instead of going further North!"

Damian grunted his agreement, then slapped his bicep with a loud "Hah!" A smear of his own blood marked the spot an insect had occupied moments before. "Dammit. Too late."

They all breathed sighs of relief when they reached woodland. The hike through the forest was pleasant and, refreshed, they reached the campsite by early evening. A small shop offered essentials, and a large, roofed area provided shelter from the Scottish weather and opportunities to mix and mingle.

Having encountered just a handful of fellow hikers all day, they headed straight there after setting up camp, looking forward to some company. But soon, Kayleigh's face scrunched up with worry.

Around half the people dotted around the tables were scratching their skin or looking visibly uncomfortable and staring at bite marks.

"Christ," she said. "Look at them. Just like that girl in the bar!"

"Do you want to go and help?" Mike asked, looking similarly worried.

"Honestly, I don't know what I can do without access to a pharmacy. I'll sleep on it. At least we're one day's walk closer to civilization."

The friends ate in silence. Between grey skies, stuffy air, clouds of midges and fungal infections, this holiday was not off to the best start.

Screams woke them just before dawn. They crawled out of their tent and, torches in hand, joined other campers in walking towards the noise. Kayleigh slapped yet another midge that had somehow found an area on her leg free of both pyjamas and insect repellent.

A man stood outside his tent, surrounded by friends unsuccessfully shielding him from view. He had stripped naked. Rash and blood covered him from head to toe. He screamed as he continued to scratch himself bloody.

Kayleigh got to "Let me have a look, I'm a do—", but she was too late. He stopped scratching, and his body went rigid, his gaze fixed on the people closest to him. He threw himself at them with a terrifying howl, his nails now tearing at their skin instead of his own. *Potentially transferring the blood on his fingers and whatever causes that rash with it,* Kayleigh thought. *Shit.*

The attack only lasted seconds before a distant look came into his eyes. He turned around, then sprinted away through the dark.

His friends went after him, but returned empty-handed half an hour later. An ambulance, they said, was on the way, but they might need to call for a rescue team to locate their patient.

Kayleigh, Mike, and Damian knew that there was no way they could go back to sleep after this. They packed up and left at first light, heading towards Loch Rannoch, away from other people and their rashes.

As they walked out of the campsite, they encountered a young woman near the remains of a bonfire. She was pressing the glowing end of a stick on the rash on her legs, and her chest was heaving with sobs. An older woman had broken into the campsite shop and raided the freezers, holding frozen peas and ice cream against her face. A man with a hipster moustache was using his Leatherman tool to cut into his arms.

Anything to make the itching stop, Kayleigh thought. She wanted to help them but did not know how. She could only make sure that her friends were safe, get them out of here before the next person went into attack mode.

Three hours later, they approached Loch Rannoch. Clouds still hung low over Perthshire, making the lush, green grass appear dull and depressing. The omnipresent clouds of midges thickened the closer they got to the water.

As soon as they reached the loch, they found the first body. A woman, naked like the people at the campsite. Her legs anchored her to the riverbank, but her hips, chest and head lay in the water, quivering eerily in the breeze.

There were more bodies. One of them was the man from the campsite, the man Kayleigh had been trying to help. His body floated on the lake, *shedding spores back into the water, closing the cycle. The midges!* A cold fist closed around her heart.

"We need to go back", she said.

"Go back?" Mike was panicking. "Are you insane? We need to get away!"

She did not have the time, patience, or energy to explain that a fungus was infecting insects, spreading through human hosts and driving them to suicide, thereby releasing its spores back into standing water, where the next generation of larvae waited.

She did not have the time because, at that exact moment, the clouds broke open and a full blast of sunshine hit them for the first time in three days.

The sun lit up emerald grass. White, pink, and brown flesh floating in the loch. Blue water. Bright red wounds left by nails desperately scratching human flesh. Red circles on the bodies in the loch. A faint red circle on Damian's arm. The grey fabric of Kayleigh's trousers covering the bite she had sustained in the night.

"Please. Let's go back. I don't think we have much time."

BIRGIT K. GAISER lives in Edinburgh, Scotland and writes short speculative fiction. They enjoy the slightly bizarre and characters who view the world with a healthy dose of sarcasm. They like to consult their PhD in toxicology for the occasional (literary) poisoning.

You can find them on Facebook (https://www.facebook.com/BirgitKGaiser) and Amazon (https://www.amazon.com/author/birgitkgaiser).

HUMMINGBIRD WHISPERS

Michael Bettendorf

"There's something wrong with the gardener," I say, and wipe sweat from my brow.

Dr. McPherson, a plant ecologist from the nearby University, stands an arm's length behind me and stares at the toolshed.

"He was slouched against the shed," I say. "At first, I thought it was heat stroke, but when I knelt down to get a closer look—"

"That's when you saw it?" Dr. McPherson asks.

"Yes," I say. "He had a beard of moss, green as lime Jell-O, and clematis grew from his eye sockets. Petals drooled onto his lap."

Dr. McPherson brushes past me and with gloved hands picks up one of the vibrant pink petals, still glowing ominously despite being off the vine. She places it carefully into a plastic bag.

"So, where's the gardener now," she asks, staring at the empty patch of flattened grass.

"I don't know?"

"Well, shit," she says. "You ought to fix that."

Dr. McPherson said she'd call from an unknown number when she learned anything. It's only been a few hours since she took the sample, but I'm antsy. My yard radiates iridescent pinks and blues and greens in lustrous dominance. Spores cover the trees like knobby pockmarks. The air smells sickly sweet and I can't stop sweating.

I fill a cup from the tap and drink. The water is no longer clear, but weak-Chamomile green.

My phone vibrates in my pocket. A text from my brother.

What the fuck did you do?

I'm not sure what I could say that would be sufficient. I type *I'm sorry*, but delete it and leave him on read. I fill a bottle of water and walk through the yard. Snails glow electric yellow and munch on mutated grass and decaying leaves. The neighbor's dog barks and barks at the vines overtaking their fence. The foxgloves dangle and I swear they lean toward me as I make for the back gate. The house, the garden—it is no longer mine. I don't think it ever was.

Soon, the barking stops.

It wasn't supposed to happen this way. To get out of hand like this. But intention didn't mean anything anymore. I wasn't a scientist. I didn't even work in the lab. I was just a custodian with dreams of creating something beautiful. When you cleanse the world with harsh chemicals for a living, picking up trash doesn't feel like enough. I wanted to do more. I wanted change, so I started stealing seed from the lab. At first it was local seed, indigenous plants to help the pollinators thrive. But the pulsing pink seeds were too tantalizing not to take.

So I cleaned while waiting for the lab assistants to leave, and took a handful of seeds out with the garbage.

It's been another hour and still no word from Dr. McPherson.

I decide to walk toward campus to look for the gardener, following a trail of pink petals. I know Dr. McPherson said not to touch them— not until she knew more about them—but they call to me. They speak my name in hummingbird whispers. They tell me things like it's *not my fault. It was inevitable.* I pick one up and it is velvet between my fingers. Silky alien skin. The veins move and spell out words and although I cannot read them, I understand what they say. I can feel their meaning. It is chaos. It is growth. And it is good.

They thank me. The gardener thanks me.

I reach the edge of campus. It is quiet. It is empty, but not barren. The students, gone home for the summer, are replaced by saplings calling out to me.

The old road, the one paved with cobblestones that leads to the environmental sciences building, is lined with native White Oaks. They no longer stand straight, but hunch like broken backs to embrace one another, forming a living tunnel. The tunnel is a throat, and it coughs leaves onto me as I walk. They land on me and stick to the sap oozing from my pores. They speak to the petal still pinched between my fingers. Words of cultivation, of conquest.

Sirens blare in the distance, inorganic cries for help, but choke to shallow gasps—silenced by the turbulent flutter of butterfly wings patterned with alien geometry.

I see a figure hobbling toward the environmental sciences building and I recognize its gait. The gardener is returning home.

Phone call.

"Hello?" I ask, but they don't understand me.

"Ryan," Dr. McPherson's voice says.

"Yes," I say. "It's me," but we no longer speak the same language.

"Ryan, call me when you get this," she says. "We found something… it's about the cellular structure of the sample."

She explains to me the differences between animal and plant cells. A lesson in basic shapes, like I am a child.

"This… this," Dr. McPherson's voice stutters, from nerves or scientific discovery I am unsure, but it is unlike her. I have listened in on her lectures. Her poise is gone. Her self-assuredness wavers like a willow in the wind.

"This is something completely different," she goes on. "It's sort of a hybrid. Plant *and* animal. It's marvelous."

I tell her we are marvelous, but she does not reply.

I reach the opulent, heavy hard-wood doors to the environmental sciences building and wonder which one of my ancestors was cut down to create such a door. I pause and run my fingers along the wood grain and feel its pain.

"…fascinating…" Dr. McPherson is saying.

I follow the petals up the stairs to the third floor where Dr. McPherson's lab is located. My feet drag along the linoleum floors I used to strip, seal, and wax. Too slick to put down roots, I carry onward. The petals beckon me.

"Ryan," Dr. McPherson says. "You've done something incredible. You need to come to the lab."

I say that I am, but she speaks as if I am not here, continuing her message.

She tells me I am the first person to get the seeds to grow.

"I don't understand how you were able to get them to flourish," she says.

The gardener is at the door now. The mutated clematis growing from his eyes grips the door knob and opens it. She doesn't scream, but I hear an echo of heavy breaths through both my phone and the doorway. I drop my phone as I reach the door. I tell her the seeds only needed the conditions to grow. The right soil. The right host.

She stares at me because she doesn't understand.

But soon, she will.

MICHAEL BETTENDORF's (he/him) work has appeared in a handful of places in print/around the internet and he is a 2021 BOTN nominee. He enjoys prog-rock a little too much and often thinks of his life as a concept album, but his dog Clover and partner love him anyway. Find him at michaelbettendorfwrites.com.

THE FOREST'S HANDMAIDEN

Stephanie M. Wytovich

In the dirt, I writhe
awakened, spoiled,
the beetles and worms
a barrier against the ivy
growing between
my eyes.

I take a breath, inhale,
there are stones in my throat,
this stagnant bloat
of decomp and well water,
my stomach a stale river,
a dead fish.

My hands break, bleed

each finger a network

of roots, chains, my body

the handmaiden to

poison and thorns,

each birth a garden,

a mandrake, a forest

inside of me

that won't stop growing

teeth.

STEPHANIE M. WYTOVICH *is an American poet, novelist, and essayist. Her Bram Stoker Award-winning poetry collection,* Brothel, *earned a home with Raw Dog Screaming Press alongside* Hysteria: A Collection of Madness, Mourning Jewelry, An Exorcism of Angels, Sheet Music to My Acoustic Nightmare, *and most recently,* The Apocalyptic Mannequin. *Her debut novel,* The Eighth, *is published with Dark Regions Press.*

Follow Wytovich on her blog at http://stephaniewytovich.blogspot.com/, on Twitter @SWytovich, and at her website stephaniemwytovich.com/.

GLASSWORK TORNADO

Katherine Silva

"Did you hear the warnings, Mrs. Shaw?"

Gabriel's voice claws its way through my thoughts like a frightened animal. I lift my head, my thoughts scattering into the recesses of my brain as I try to figure out what he's talking about. Ah, yes. The report that had played across the radio, the man's voice scratched and pitchy. He didn't want to "alarm" anyone. His voice did that on its own. Had it only been minutes ago? Before the electricity fizzled out, and the cold began to seep in from all sides...

"What should we do?" Emily spoke next. There was distress in the question, an escalation that settled across everyone in the room. Their breathing strained and skipped and sobs rose from the gathering like the sounds of scared rabbits. I reached for my mobility stick, where it should have been, but my hand met with the rough surface of the desk drawer. A spike of panic. Where? What had I—*Oh, there it is.* My grip tightened around the rubber handle.

"Settle down." My voice maintains an illusion of calm, one that seems to stifle the hiccupping anguish from the class in front of me.

"We are going to leave the classroom. We will walk down the hall in pairs. Each one of you is responsible for the person beside you. We're going to go down to the cellar and wait until the storm is over."

"It's not a storm," an angry voice protests. It takes me longer than it should to identify who it belongs to. Travis. Troublemaker. Picks on the younger boys in class. "It's a tornado."

"Maine doesn't get bad tornados," I answer, automatically. "It'll most likely be some heavy wind and rain. We'll be more than safe in the cellar." My false confidence somehow reassures me.

"It's going to destroy the school!" another child screams. The others start clamoring again. I feel a small hand slip into mine and for an instant, my memories go off like fireworks. I see her deep brown eyes. The decadent pink confetti cake with frosting like cumulus and splotches of chocolate ice cream dotting her new purple dress. The small flare in the dim evening of the candle shaped like a six.

"Mrs. Shaw?" Lily's voice. I'm back here in the school. "Are we going to die?"

Words that should never be said by a child. Words that I want to scrape like old paint out of my ears they moment they land. I fight the thickness in my throat as I say, "No. Not today. We're gonna be fine."

I stand from my chair, my feet feel the pins and needles of inactivity. I orchestrate the class to gather in a line, two by two. Their chairs screech across the linoleum as they stand, as their sneakers scuff into place before me. I count the footsteps and I ask for them to sound off, which they do in varying emotions from fright to bother. I take my place at the head of the line. How I wish my aide hadn't called in sick today. I want someone at the rear, someone who can see what they're doing, someone who could make sure they all stayed in line…

I twist the knob and we walk into the hall.

The schoolhouse is tiny. One class on the island, one class with several ages. It's all the town can afford and it's exactly what I needed: an escape. The school is three rooms: my classroom nestled toward the water side of the building where the sun plays across the crayon art in the early afternoon; the administrator's office which is empty on account of Mr. Branson taking a meeting on the mainland; and the alternative classroom, the one we use to take the little ones away for naptime while the older ones learn more complex lessons.

I was told the building was covered in windows. While I can't see them, I have imagined their view time and time again, the hazy sun blistering over an open ocean and craggy shoreline, and have felt the warmth of it caress my skin day after day, even in winter. Today, wind seeps in like fingers. I can hear it knocking against the sides of the building, wobbling against the glass. I can still hear the sound of it breaking, like ice crackling on a pond.

It takes eight footsteps to reach the door to the cellar. This didn't exist when the building was built, there wasn't even a foundation. A group of men could have thrown a rope around it and dragged it away if they'd wanted. Someone eventually saw the error. Children need a safe place to go in case of an emergency. The island doesn't have a community center or a bunker. The ferry comes twice a day: today not at all because of the weather.

The cellar: I'd been shown where it was once when I started teaching. Mr. Branson had walked me to the door, he'd taken my hand in his and shown me where the light switch was. I'd descended the stairs and felt cold clamminess swell across my skin.

I remembered rain and the taste of copper in my nose. I remembered voices calling across the sky and the fury of the storm wailing all around me. My heartbeat thunders in strange parts of my skull. Our home was toothpicks. Our blankets, quilts, and warm garments were saturated, and she was gone, stolen by the wind.

I realize that these unfathomable sounds are not just in my memory; they cut across the white caps and the stratified rocks like a banshee. The scream is nonsensical; brazen even. It streams through my consciousness as though it has always been there, like it's followed me...

I opened the cellar door, flicked on the light with a trembling finger. The darkness pulses against my body and her voice calls to me from inside it. She's still singing the Happy Birthday song.

The tornado was a rarity, they told me, as I picked through wreckage, searching for fragments of my life before. EF-4. They don't happen up here. There would likely never be another in my lifetime.

An anomaly, they had said.

They had lied.

The schoolhouse shudders around us. Debris scrapes and buzzes against the roof.

The earth is no longer the same as it was when I was a child. It's unpredictable. It bristles with vengeance. It's not safe.

These ideals sent my husband away. He had been sold on the idea of an anomaly, maybe because it hurt too much to think that the earth had done this to our daughter. He wanted to believe it was nothing.

It's not nothing.

"Mrs. Shaw?"

I turn to my class. "It's all right. There's nothing to be afraid of."

The glass is singing in the window. I can imagine the tornado gyrating forward, body pinning back and forth across the uneven landscape. An abysmal cloud of rubble shields its shredding teeth.

"I'll keep you safe."

One by one, they step down into the blackness.

KATHERINE SILVA is a two-time Maine Literary Award finalist for speculative fiction. She's a member of the Horror Writers of Maine, the Maine Writers and Publishers Alliance, and New England Horror Writers Association. Her latest book, The Wild Dark, *is available for pre-order and comes out October 12th, 2021. More can be found about her at katherinesilvaauthor.com.*

MOONLIGHT OVER THE GARDEN DOVES

Steven Lombardi

He would call her his pretty little dove, though she loathed the pet name. It seemed too aware of its own cruelty. What is a dove in one's possession, if not a pretty thing in a cage, singing songs of salvation as if to magic its cage open? For five years, she served that title well, being a beautiful creature draped over his shoulder. But with each year, the love and the promise of things that last cooled until they strangled her in place like icy fingers.

Of course, she made excuses for him. Why would she be unable to see her friends, unless he wanted to spend every waking moment with her? Why would he say damning things about her clothes, unless he wanted her to look her best? And why would he raise his hand to her, unless he loved her so fiercely that it transcended all boundaries of the physical?

It was the marks on her arms and an unplanned visit from her sister that set her escape in motion. The cage had finally been unlocked, and, like a long-starved creature, she limped away from her captor.

Her sister said they needed to escape the city. Not only for physical safety, but for emotional rejuvenation. They packed enough clothes for a week and retreated to the family's country house, replacing recent memory with warm reminiscence. Their bedrooms were just as they left them, still well-maintained by their parents. The fields and the mountains were unchanged, as was the town's main street. The local pub they had passed on so many nights when they were children now glowed as if to welcome them in. And both sisters agreed that they could use a drink.

The men in the pub were old and mild, which seemed the very antithesis of her former lover, and in that she found peace. But there was one who stood out in the crowd. He had curly hair and vibrant green eyes, and an easy way of sipping his beer as he stole glances at the sisters.

"Just ignore him," her sister said. "You need time to be alone."

But was that true? She wasn't stupid—she understood what abuse was when it hovered over her jaw in a tightened fist. Still, she did not flee her cage, even when the door was left open. Why would she? The fear of pain was nothing compared to the fear of loneliness.

"What harm is there in finding out his name?"

Her sister rolled her eyes and groaned.

I'm Drake, he said, *like mandrake*. Not the kind you'd find at the local nursery, but the ancient kind. The kind that would scream when you dug them out of the ground.

He chuckled and sipped his beer, and all she could smell was the alcohol and the earthy odor lingering off his shirt. When he mentioned his mother's shop across the street, which sold herbs and stones and honey, she felt her heart open with trust. She had always loved that shop. Her sister, on the other hand, despised the old woman who tended the till. She said the old woman's eyes never moved in unison, and that she was always too eager to laugh.

When the hour was late, he left the bar, but not without exchanging numbers. She insisted. Her sister said she was wasting her time, but she wasn't getting any younger, nor prettier, nor better from the emotional wear, so did she really have the luxury of time?

The sisters switched from beer to wine at the house, and her sister teased her with information she found about the mandrake.

"Used as a narcotic. How charming," her sister said. "Oh. Here it says mandrake is a hallucinogen. People believed it could make them fly. But that's the thing with hallucinogens—none of it is real."

"If you believe in something enough, then it's as good as real," she insisted.

She dreamt of him that night. He drank beer in the bar, wearing a button-up shirt with a pattern of purple bell-shaped corollas. His skin was the color of soil, and warm as if sunned, and in his mouth was a green leaf in place of a tongue, and when she kissed it, she flew. It was such a silly dream, yet it awoke her in the night, the butterflies rattling in her stomach. The buzz of the wine made her head swim, and against her better judgement, she sent him a text at an ungodly hour.

He was probably sleeping. But who knows? A girl can dream. And as she had argued with her sister, she wasn't *dependent* on anyone. She just liked the way people could fill the many holes and chambers of her heart. Call it an addiction. She saw no danger in it, not like the witches of old who were addicted to the effects of mandrake.

She awoke again that night before the sun had risen. At first she thought something in the house had fallen off a shelf, as old houses tended to drop things. But it came again, a more deliberate sound. Someone knocking on the door. When she looked through the window, she saw him standing in his purple flower shirt, holding a large bouquet of flowers. It was still before 5 a.m., and she knew better than to answer the door. But only at first. Because why would he be up so late, unless he'd been rolling in bed thinking of their evening together? Why would he come so eagerly, unless he saw a future for the two of them? And why would he bring a bouquet of her favorite flowers, having no prior knowledge of this, unless they were two souls destined to intertwine?

He apologized for coming at such a late hour. The earthy fragrance coming off his body was as potent as a field of lavender. It soothed her, even lured her in. She knew she shouldn't enter his car, but a gnawing at her heart said it would be okay. And as they drove along the unpaved mountain roads, she saw colors in the fields that she didn't know existed. The trees moved in sync, but not by the wind's doing, and the flowers sprouted eyes to look upon her, as if she was their queen, and he was their king. Her heart fluttered, her breath quickening.

"What's happening?" she asked.

"You're flying," Drake said. And as he spoke, his tongue moved, only it resembled something green and leafy. His skin turned the color of soil, bits of it crumbling from his hands as he turned the steering wheel. And she wanted to scream. She wanted to roll out of the car and run. But all she could do was laugh uncontrollably, just like the old woman who tended the tills at the naturalist shop.

"You'll be okay," Drake said. She had heard that line before and knew it was a lie, but every attempt to cry or scream turned into explosive laughter.

He parked outside his house. Or was it a cave? The world blurred together in strange colors, and the vegetation kept moving, as if caught in a fevered dance, making it impossible to make sense of what was before her. He led her inside, where darkness awaited. Sharp stones cut her feet and jammed her toes, but all she could do was laugh some more.

"Please don't kill me," she said, laughing hysterically.

He led her towards a halo of light, where the cave opened overhead to let the moonlight in, and she saw the others. All women, all different ages, stood in gnarled wooden planters. They all laughed at her when she stepped under the light of the moon, tears streaming down their faces. Drake picked her up around the waist and set her into a planter. Her blood and the soil mixed, and roots sprouted from her wounds, twisting into the dirt as if to never let go.

She tried to move her legs but couldn't, and she looked desperately to the moon for help, but it could not decipher the meaning of her laughter, no more than she could understand the other women.

When Drake left his garden of pretty things, she tried to dig herself free, but the roots of her feet had hardened into the shape of the planter. Yet she did find a rock, slender and smooth and sharp. In her mind, beneath the laughter and mania, she heard a voice call to her, saying, *My pretty little dove.*

When doves get their wings clipped, they lose their sense of freedom. But for this little dove, clipping her wings was the only means of escape.

As she brought the edge of the stone down across her ankle, sawing through the skin, she couldn't help but laugh.

STEVEN LOMBARDI lives in New York City with his wife and daughter. A copywriter by day, author by night, he received his Bachelor of Arts in screenwriting from the School of Visual Arts. In February 2021, he won the Dark Sire *award for best fiction. You can find his work at stevenlombardi.nyc.*

GIFTS

Charlotte Reynolds

They wash up on my shores
    more and more these days,
      limp and anaemic creatures
    of feather and scale,
  skeleton grey
except for the bright jewels
    that bulge from their stomachs,
      bottle caps, pen lids, bread tags,
     bendy straws, spoons and plastic bags,
  their flesh soon melts into my sand
but the plastic, oh, your plastic,
    stays radiant in everlasting colour

I have been thinking it over,
    rolling your buoyant gifts
     in my briny hands,
    licking the thick chemical skin
  that glistens on my surface,
you have given me so much,
    but it is time to return the treasures
     you have emptied into my mouths
    my children, be patient,
  give me a few years
and I will be lapping at your door
    with more than you can bear

CHARLOTTE REYNOLDS is an analyst from London. She has poetry featured in or is forthcoming in Briefly Zine, Tattie Zine *and* Kalopsia Lit. *You can find her on Twitter @violetvicinity.*

AND THE CALCIUM CHIMES WILL SWAY

Hazel Ragaire

Towards the beginning of the end, no one realized what would happen. Well, maybe the biologists knew; after all, in the early twenty-first century they'd proved that of the four billion species that once called earth home, ninety-nine percent were extinct. Over nine hundred species in the last five centuries alone: outright slaughter, habitat destruction, trophy hunting, exotic pet trade. Human indifference and arrogance resulted in a near-planetary species extinction at the end. And yet humans continued to build and take and raze.

I remember the news announcements of rolling extinctions; in a single week the axolotl, Amur leopard, bluefin tuna, Bornean orangutan, dugong, greater sage-grouse, Sunda tiger, and vaquita all disappeared. The thought of nature rising against us never occurred to anyone. Yet it happened. Whether the natural world was always sentient and held out hope for us eventually didn't matter; what mattered was that nature rose up universally, in a single instant enacting a simple plan: do unto them as they have done unto us.

One Tuesday evening we all went to bed. We streamed our favorite shows, brushed our teeth, burrowed under weighted blankets, and tried not to think about the ravens' arrival. For days they'd descended upon the cities worldwide, lining roofs like well-placed rooks. Waiting. Baffled ornithologists expressed grave concern over such undocumented behavior. They cautioned the public to avoid rooftops completely, but few listened, insisting they paid good money for rooftop lounges and pools and exclusive open-air restaurants with three-hundred-and-sixty degree views. The rock-throwers found themselves swarmed, pecked, bleeding, and blind. The sharpshooters hit their targets but suffered the same fate; there were just so many. The arrival continued and blackened the skies.

So we stayed away from the roofs.

Days later, strange reports flooded the news sites: ancient trees were moving. Governments dispatched dendrologists globally to study the impossibility of such a reality. Arborists joined in, certain the trees had been axed and harmed in some unprecedented prank. Newsreels showed the trees sliding through the dirt as if it were water. Wary, people waited, but they didn't know for what.

The Arbol del Tule in Oaxaca shivered its branches and the stone streets groaned as it razed paths demolishing brightly colored buildings. The two-thousand-year-old Montezuma Cypress carved its way through the city, crushing everything it could with its one hundred and thirty-eight foot width.

The Cotton Tree in Sierra Leone destroyed one hundred and seventy-one buildings before resting just outside its city.

The Major Oak in Nottinghamshire moved *towards* London. Paved roads buckled under its twenty-three tons. Brick and mortar buildings fell from its ninety-two foot branch span.

The Avenue of the Baobabs in Madagascar moved as a unit, surrounding the capital city Antananarivo.

Jaya Sri Maha Bodhi in Sri Lanka danced its way to the city's center, roots digging deep along the roadways, rerouting traffic for days.

The Dragon Blood trees in the Socotra archipelago left their island and walked onto Yemen's shores and moved towards Sana'a bringing the ocean with them, drowning people in their wake.

General Sherman in California stayed put.

But the Cedars of God, the last four hundred in the world, shocked everyone by leaving Lebanon and arriving in Egypt, mummies coated in their resin littering their path.

Finally, the Boab Prison Tree arrived in Perth, decimating the Great National highway, ominously settling before the mouth of the city. Those who got too close found themselves entombed, as the tree resurrected its history but as perpetrator rather than a bystander.

Humans snapped images, posting selfies with the trees. Officials scrambled, assessing damage to road and underground infrastructure, debating the best retaliatory approach with the least casualties. The ravens just waited.

That night, clouds unfurled in the sky blotting out all light and we went to bed certain to discover what was happening tomorrow. We missed the growing sounds of cement crumbing: crackling followed by stones grating upon each other with a nearly indiscernible sound of rustling leaves. Potholes yawned wide; cracks became gaping maws.

The homeless woke, marveled at the reclamation, and died pierced where they sat, blood trails dripping steadily as their bodies rose, spasming.

Alarms blaring, others woke, worked out, brewed coffee, exited their buildings eyes glued to their phones and died screaming, impaled.

Crucifixions, just without the nails.

We woke to see hundreds of thousands of trees below us, waiting with branches beckoning, bloodied rag dolls hanging. And we left our buildings en-masse to gawk at the Ents, armed with whatever we had. And they ran us through. Branches reached through the bodies as if they were warmed butter, gaping holes widening under the weight. Red rivers slogged through the road debris, turning rust then black under the sun's heat. Millions hung, skewered through the chest or torso, the brain or groin.

Before the electricity stopped and the internet died, I googled how many trees remained on the planet: over three trillion. That's over four hundred trees per person. Those were never good odds; nothing left of the Spartan spirit runs through us now. We couldn't kill them quickly enough; I'm not actually sure we killed any of them. Bullets did little. Fire scarred but didn't stop them; it just made our deaths more gruesome. They lined every road, street, and alley we'd ever paved; they encircled the cities and took their time in the country. They weren't fast but final. They came for us, and we *knew*. Starvation and madness drove us from our homes to waiting death, eventually. In the end, I watched as some just walked out toward the trees.

How often did we pluck a flower and put it in our hair? The elms and oaks and ash and cypress and yew and tamboti and banyan and willow and sequoia and baobab didn't pluck us for our beauty.

They splayed their branches, inviting the ravens to feast. The vultures and rats followed, munching through tendons and organs. The bugs blossomed, arriving in hordes to enjoy us to the bone. Vines wove among and between sun-bleaching bones. Humanity's skeletons jigged in the wind, phalanges and tibia jerking helter-skelter.

And I? I waited as long as I could survive indoors. Long past scavenging for resources, resolutely I left what I knew behind. I left everything behind. I walked into the sun, Eve in the garden, sun-starved skin burning. Hands before me holding plants I'd nurtured, I prostrated.

Hair now gray, I wander the world, stepping carefully wherever I go. Breaking apart pine cones, I throw their seeds into the wind; I place acorns beneath the earth in sunny patches. Always, I hear the knocking of calcium chimes above me, and I record what I know, what I witness, and what I discover. Arriving in California, thriving Marbled Murrelet communities centered around General Sherman; he stayed to shelter them. The world recovers without us. The trees tower above our crumbled buildings and dwarf our monuments. Alone, I spread their seeds and live.

Only ideas outnumber the books in HAZEL RAGAIRE's home. When she's not conjuring up new worlds, you'll likely find her plotting. Her favorite word is airneán, and you're welcome to join her online at www.hazelragaire.com or @HRagaire on Twitter to explore published or in-progress stories.

TRANSPLANT

Tonya Walter

The studio apartment is a forest. Lush green fern fronds stretch from the green shape of a bed to the popcorn-textured ceiling. Smaller, curlicued stalks sprout from soft moss that grows over the beige carpet. A limp hand and the corner of a paisley sheet dangle out from beneath thick tangles of plant roots.

In Lauren's final moments, she could feel the plant taking from her body, draining vital nutrients even as it filled her lungs and pumped her heart.

"You found me," she whispered, and the fern whispered back in a language without words, humming through her veins. In the end, Lauren smiled and ran a finger over its paper-thin leaves, closing her eyes, carried away by its song and the smell of ocean air. In the end, she was warm and no longer afraid of living or dying or…

Waking suddenly, Lauren felt a gentle tugging through her veins, akin to the peeling of healing sunburns, the pull of old, translucent skin sloughing from the new. Lauren sat up and a hot, biting pain screamed through her body. She pushed at the potted fern beside her but it stuck. Roots wormed down her bloodstream, becoming a part of her, and she wished she'd left the plant to freeze, left it...

On the nightstand, the fern drooped, wilted, defeated by the cold.

"I'm sorry," she murmured.

Lauren put the plastic pot beside her on the mattress and breathed into its tendrils, the only comfort she could offer. The power went out on the same night a cold snap descended. She knew it was coming; the power outage. She hadn't checked the forecast but she had checked the mail, had received the pink overdue notices. When her thermostat gave a quiet, final tick, she didn't bother getting up to investigate. She stayed in bed, breathing in the damp earth scent and remembering the news...

She heard on the radio, delivered in acres per minute, the speed at which her hometown was burning away. She eyed the fern on the nightstand. A single fern can spread into a colony, she'd read. Could this plant sense its colony the way amputees feel their lost limbs? Was it groping in the dark for a body a thousand miles away? Could it feel the fire? Lauren reminded herself that, as much as it looked like the coastal ferns from her childhood, it might not have come from the seaside at all. Her fern could be from Mexico, or the Florida swamplands, for all she knew. There was no reason to assume it had made its way to a Mid-Western Home Depot from the West Coast's Redwood Forests, that it had traveled a thousand miles away...

From the forest floor where Lauren lay, she could hear the soft babble of conversation, the crescendo of a set-up and the bass thump of a punchline. Laughter. Fern leaves tickled her face and, with eyes closed, she imagined a strong, steady heartbeat pulsing through the soil. A warm glow swelled as her friends stoked the campfire. In the morning, she'd be on her way to a fresh start a thousand miles from here and her pile of wrecked relationships but now, lying in the ferns, the sky above was more stars than dark and Lauren tried to preserve the moment so she could carry it with her...

Down a slope covered in knee-high tendrils, Lauren trudged. Thick, white mist shrouded the ground and devoured her from the knees down. It looked cold and damp, the fog, but it was warm. Lauren walked until her boyfriend and her mother and the questions about the car, and the money, and the drinking, couldn't find her. She sat on a carpet of dead leaves, head rising just above the sea of green. She remembered the thing she'd read: these ferns were all genetically identical. They sprouted from the same rhizome and emerged from the soil, pretending to be individuals, instead of polyps on an ancient giant's back. All different faces of the same thing, all but the one. She got up and marched toward it, crunchy, brown, and diseased. Lauren plunged her fingers into the soft earth, tearing roots, pulling, twisting, until something ripped and the plant came away from the colony.

Staring at the marred, disrupted soil, she felt the gravity of her mistake. She pressed the mess of vegetation into the dark dirt, mashing roots to earth. She couldn't fix it. For now, for the first time, it was alone.

Formerly a ghost writer of Child Safety pamphlets and Pagan Witchcraft guidebooks, TONYA WALTER now writes short stories about a wide variety of nightmares and insect-centric flash fiction. Bits of her fiction and weird art live at thefictitioustonyawalter.com. She is a tweeter, @fictitioustw, and an occasional contributor to the Vine Leaves Press opinion column SPILL IT!

PLANTS CAN'T SCREAM

D. R. Roberts

"Yes!"

Rayan had asked me if I had stubbed my joint out properly for the hundredth time. Her fiery Latin nature was not going to settle for any of the vague answers I gave before. She aimed her eyes back at the TV, gulping on her bottle of Rolling Rock.

It was hot in the hostel common room. Or, at least, it felt hot.

We were watching the fires burning on the news. Three days and two-hundred thousand acres of actionable woodland turned to black.

Three days.

Three days earlier, we'd been there. We all liked nature. Took a few cases of beer, Mike brought his guitar, about a quart of not overly strong weed, built a campfire, sang Kumbaya and shit. We all forgot our lives for one night. It was cool.

They said on the news it was the heatwave, so I don't know why Rayan kept looking at me. Truth is, I flicked a stub into a patch of grass. I'm pretty sure it was out. Pretty sure.

The fire continued to burn for the next few weeks. The media got their pound of flesh from it, along with the doomsday bells of climate change. It became meme-worthy, and did the rounds on late-night talk shows, the punchline to so many zeitgeist jokes.

Two months later, it was nearly burnt out, but not before destroying over a million acres of wood and grassland. Vast stocks of wildlife were lost, including the wiping out of three endangered species. But by then we had all moved on, lost interest. We took note, sure, but then got back to our timelines and our feeds.

The next bit of news in that area didn't make as much of a splash. Not at first.

It was the regrowth.

Why was that even remotely newsworthy, anyway? It was the speed. Within four days, an abundance of greenery, foliage and flowers had exploded into life, reclaiming the land that had only just burnt away. And ground zero of this sudden proliferation? The very spot we'd set up camp all those weeks ago.

I was in a bar with Tony Trees, our regular supplier of weed. He'd been with us that night, and when we saw ground zero of the regrowth we'd just looked at one another. He may have even raised an eyebrow, which was the equivalent of full-blown hysterics for Tony. I was just glad Rayan wasn't there with her accusatory looks.

Anyway it wasn't a big deal. It was a quirk of nature. The land more fertile from the ash, blah, blah, blah, right?

No. Not so. For the growth kept growing. Beyond the borders of the fire zone. And faster too. It overtook farmlands, grew through tarmac roads, even climbed up telegraph wires.

It was inconvenient at first. Roads blocked, telephone lines down, but then it started to get real creepy.

Our little group had kind of been moving North anyway, so we were far from all the happenings, and when I heard this story, I was so glad of that

A family of five. Mom, Dad, a little girl, nine, and twin boys, both seven. They had gone to bed that night, the Growth less than a mile away. By the morning, what could be described as their house was still there. Structurally, it looked the same. But the walls and roof were all covered in roots, vines, moss. The windows smashed through with creepers. Every surface, carpets, rugs, pieces of furniture, everything covered, taken over, consumed.

And the family. One can only hope they remained asleep. Vines and roots had punctured their skin, entwined their veins and wrapped around their bones. Most disturbing of all was their eyes. Each one of them had their eyeballs ruptured by a marigold flowering from their sockets. It was like a calling card.

They, of course, were the first of many. The flourishing expanded, more and more rapidly. As towns and villages were consumed, the government rallied to halt the Growth.

Agent Orange was used for the first time since the Vietnam war. Sure, it halted the Growth momentarily, but then it just came back. Quicker, more abundant, more verdant. More alive.

When they fire bombed L.A., it was the moment I felt we had stepped through the looking glass. It felt like we were no longer in control. The riots in Seattle weren't as bad as elsewhere, but we had to get out before the chaos overwhelmed us.

And still this verdancy was unstoppable. There was news footage of the Growth. You know those wildlife programmes you see where they show plants growing using stop-motion photography? This was the same, only the cameras were running at a normal frame rate. Scientists scratched their heads, saying it wasn't possible, that plants and trees could not grow that fast, but tell that to the people impaled on tree branches that had grown through them. Say that whilst standing amongst forests of corpses hanging from the branches, wooden lances piercing their hearts and their lungs. Some even pierced from anus to mouth. Can you believe that? And every single one had marigolds for eyes.

The sudden rout of our civilisation led to more death. People trampled, cars crashed, people murdered over rolls of toilet paper. Food ran out. Civilisation crumbled.

I was lucky. The military got us across the border to Canada. Took us to a camp, but we didn't stay. We travelled further north. If it's cold enough, things can't grow, right?

It was just five of us now. John knew about a hut up in the mountains. It had fresh water from a spring not far away; creeks nearby for fishing. It was sustainable. Tony had a mind-blowing amount of weed. We'd be good. Plus me and Rayan had brought books.

And a windup radio.

So we listened. Nearly all day, and all night. Listened to the spread, listened as everything went dark, 'till even the emergency broadcast went down.

Rayan chewed her nails, bare feet tucked up in the corner chair by the wood burner. She stared at me with her indifferent eyes. The static crackled as I fiddled with the radio. Hope had gone of hearing anything else, but it was habit now. But her staring made me turn it off and ask her, "What?"

"Was it you?"

I'm bored of this question.

I turned away from her, and rubbed a clear spot in the condensation on the window. The evergreens were white. Nothing stirred out there. Not even the wind.

No one spoke all evening. We didn't even say goodnight to one another when we went to bed.

None of them woke up. I envied them for that. When I opened my eyes in the morning light, Rayan was standing over me, her eyes filled with fire.

No, not fire.

Yellow.

Marigolds.

She was slightly suspended above the floor, held in place by branches and vines. I could see Tony Trees' face poking out of leaves on the wall. John was swinging, choking vines around his neck. The

Growth had taken them and filled the cabin everywhere. Everywhere except for a tiny, almost perfect circle around my bed.

I was trapped somewhere between a scream and choking. I thought this was it, that this was my punishment for failing to stub a joint. But it was just a prelude.

It was quick and painful, my skin punctured, my veins strangled, the sockets of my burst eyes caressed by soft petals.

I waited for it to end, for my heart to stop beating, for my brain to shut down. But it didn't. This thing, this Growth didn't kill us. It kept us alive.

A voice spoke in my head.

Isn't this wonderful?

I didn't scream.

D.R. ROBERTS lives in Kent, UK with his wife (who stalks people for fun), son (who is named after a vampire) and two fat cats (who ate all the pies). He has worked in a castle, lived on a remote island and he is also a trained chef. He loves the macabre, lighthouses and getting caught in the rain. He sometimes acts, directs and writes whenever he can find a pen. Find him at www.davidrroberts.com.

THE QUEEN OF THE NIGHT

Clay F. Johnson

Is not this the witching time of night? The waters murmur, and fall
with more than mortal music, and spirits of peace walk abroad to
calm the agitated breast. Eternity is in these moments. Worldly cares
melt into the airy stuff that dreams are made of.

—Mary Wollstonecraft

How enrapturing is the night
Whose darkness breeds eternity,
Whose voice of immortality
Speaks to me within dreams divine,
Othering me with ecstasies
Of incorporeal light

A noctilucent glamoury
Lures me to its vespertine life:
Flickering ghost-lights of fireflies,
Bioluminescent *blue ghosts*
Alive and luciferous;
The green-eyed cicadae, rising
From a grave-like sleep to sing
In swarms of unburied crypsis;
And the cooing aziola,

The watcher owl, watching
For what waits in the fading light

Seduced by night-music, nocturnes
Of unseen bewitchments, hypnotized
By wandering will-o'-wisp light
And its illusions of movement,
I trace its aerial secrets
Into the thickening darkness,
And as I creep deeper, deeper
Into the sylvan night, I find
A lifeless flower withered white

But as I watch the moon goddess
Rise sublime, I gaze with wondrous
Melting eyes as the lifeless flower
Stirs with life, night-sick and alive
It blooms beneath the moon's
Luminous gaze of lustral light

Yet, under the spell of lunacy's madness,
Not even the moon can appease
Such leafy malevolence—
A lunar-synthesis of Orphic
Metamorphosis She exists
In *other light* liminality

Diaphanously She dances
With Nature's witchery, scenting
The haunted air as Her petals bloom
With moon-cancer, a fragrance like
Vanilla orchid touched by
Phantasmal light, an aphrodisiac
For nocturnal pollinators
That sleep by day and wake all night:

The long-nosed bat flittering
In fits of nectar ecstasies,
Skeletal-fingered wings glistening

In echoes of light, unfurling
Its demon-like tongue, numb, dripping
With opium on the moon-vine,
A Dionysian smile thick with pollen
Catching the moonlight like fairy dust

And the worm-tongued sphinx moth,
White-lined, untouched by the death-mark,
Unclothed by the white-witch ghost
Whose sole frailty is deathlessness,
Yet possessed by fay-wingèd night magic
Of the owlet enchantress black witch,
Swing-hovering the opening petals
In fear of what waits with death's kiss:

In illuminated darkness She blooms,
Unveiling a pale, tendrilled creature—
On a single night Her white spider renewed,
Lustrous and twisted in delicious solitude

How enrapturing is the night
Whose darkness breeds eternity,
Whose voice of immortality
Speaks to me in dreams divine,
Othering me with ecstasies
Of incorporeal light,
And as I gaze deeper, deeper,
Ascending into visions sublime,
I melt away into the darkness
And become one with the night.

CLAY F. JOHNSON is an amateur pianist, devoted animal lover, and incorrigible reader of Gothic literature & Romantic-era poetry. His first collection of poetry, A Ride Through Faerie & Other Poems, *is forthcoming from Gothic Keats Press. Find out more on his website at www.clayfjohnson.com or follow him on Twitter @ClayFJohnson.*

MULCH

Chloe Spencer

Rose bushes so red, they seemed to glow in the auburn twilight. Every evening, just after dinner, Callie would creep over to the fence that separated her yard from Mrs. Langley's. She would stand on her swing set, shimmy up the pole, and swing her legs over the top, just so she could get a better look. Mrs. Langley would never catch her. The old woman hadn't left her house since Callie was too small to climb onto the swing set herself. Yet somehow, someway, the rose bushes were still thriving—and in Callie's young mind, that meant that they were magic.

Whenever her friends came over, they all marveled over them. They whispered amongst themselves about how Mrs. Langley, a woman who had been born almost a hundred years ago, could still be alive today. They all agreed, it had *something* to do with the roses. But tonight, for certain, Callie would find out. Her father hadn't come home for dinner again, and, in her frustration, her mother had popped a couple of her "special vitamins" in addition to a glass of wine. No one would be looking forCallie. It was the perfect time to enact her plan.

After admiring the rose bushes, Callie jumped down; the chains of the swing set rattling. She stumbled a bit, and ended up scraping her hands against the ground. Frowning, she examined her stinging hands, meddled with dirt and ruby-rose blood glistening through. She scrubbed her hands against her jeans and proceeded over to the fence. One panel, pushed out of place—narrow, but still wide enough for her to squeeze through. And so she did.

Callie stepped into the garden and immediately felt the lush, soft grasses grazing the tips of her bare toes. It was a far cry from the manicured, rough grass of her own yard. She removed her sandals and tossed them back over the fence. It felt so calm, so soothing. The rose bushes sat in the dead center of the yard, ringing around a broken-down fountain. She had seen it so many times before, and it looked so easy to get to, but now, suddenly standing in the hearty wilderness of Mrs. Langley's garden, her task seemed that much more difficult, the trees much taller, nearly obscuring her path. The branches, with their long velvety arms, scratched and scraped at her as she moseyed through.

While the pathway was unpleasant, the sights and smells enraptured her. Cherry blossoms mixed with the effervescent citrus of a lemon tree; the frosty aura of pine and gentle lavender. The rainbow of colors speckling the foliage and her pathway forward—as magical a garden as the ones in her favorite picture books.

Finally, she reached the center. The waters of the fountain were still, the open mouths of the decorative lions ferocious but rusted. Their granite eyes stared ahead lifelessly. Such a strange contrast to the beautiful roses. Although overeager, Callie knew well enough to stop and examine them. Vicious thorns lined the stems and nestled underneath the roses' bases. She bent over and inhaled their oddly sugary, fragrant smell. Luscious and rich and deep and everything that she had imagined them to be, but more. And the glow, she found, wasn't just from the light of the dying sun. They were truly alight, like little stars red and round. She carefully pinched the base of one rose and slowly twisted it off the vine. It nestled in the palm of her hands like a beating heart.

Wait.

It was beating.

Just like a heart.

Callie watched as the flower pulsated in her hands, its light strong and shimmering. Its petals felt ginger and soft, but still, panic rose inside of her. Its pulse quickened slowly, gradually building up, and she spread her shaking hands apart as if to drop it—

"Stop!"

Callie's head jerked upwards as she searched for the voice. Then she saw her: Mrs. Langley, standing on the steps of her porch. Even though it was the dead of summer, she wore a turtleneck that curled up underneath her knobby chin, and a floor-length skirt that spilled over the splintered top step. She looked comically small in her oversized clothes; almost Hobbit-like. Her skin was near translucent but vaguely rosy; her eyes a dead-fish blue and intensely angry.

"What do you think you're doing?"

Callie stammered nonsensically in response. She attempted to drop the rosebud again, but Mrs. Langley's sharp *tut-tut* stopped her. Callie remained frozen, her hands outstretched. The old woman placed her hands on her hips.

"What are you doing in my yard? Where do you come from?"

"I'm your neighbor?" Callie was surprised. Sure, they had never met in person, but she hadn't anticipated that the woman wouldn't know her completely.

The old woman glanced over at the house next door with a dissatisfied expression. "*Oh.* Yes. You're the nosy one who's always spying into my backyard with your friends. Clearly you're being raised by wolves, as your parents haven't taught you any manners."

"I'm sorry!" Callie blurted. "Your roses! T-they were just so pretty, and—"

"—They are quite beautiful. But still." She clicked her tongue again, shaking her head. She proceeded down the steps of her porch, and approached Callie. "You should really ask for permission before doing something so rude." Her fingers delicately brushed against the petals and she smiled gingerly at Callie, as if something inside her had softened. But Callie still felt too afraid to let the rosebud drop.

"I was worried that if I asked you wouldn't let me in," Callie explained. She looked over towards the horizon at the setting sun. The roses were still glowing and pulsating even though the light was largely gone. "I-I wanted to learn the secret to growing such beautiful roses."

"Oh? Have you a bit of a green thumb?" Mrs. Langley continued to stroke the petals of the individual flowers, almost absentmindedly.

"I'd like to. Maybe one day. Whenever my parents will let me." Callie scrunched up her nose, which was starting to itch, but she wouldn't dare move her hands to scratch it.

"So why were you so interested in my roses?"

"W-well… it's silly."

"Say it." Mrs. Langley's gaze sharpened. "You have the audacity to break in, and you won't tell me, child?"

"M-my friends and I—Stacy and Becca—I mean, you're one of the oldest ladies we've ever known. And w-we thought that you've lived as long as you did because your garden was magic." Callie's cheeks and ears burned with embarrassment as she realized how childish she sounded. Her voice warbled as she spoke. "It's stupid."

Mrs. Langley chuckled, much to her surprise. Callie nervously laughed as well.

"Well, you're right. My garden is my secret." she smiled politely at the girl. "And it is magic."

"Really?"

"Not in the way that you would expect." Mrs. Langley pointed at her feet.

Callie blinked in confusion and looked down. She saw the grass—so soft before, but now so brittle, curling tightly around her feet and ankles. She tried to move, but she was fixed in place. She grunted and tried to pull her foot free, but the grasses grew longer, weaving their way around her ankle; slowly inching upward. With each centimeter they crept, Callie felt sicker and sicker.

Panicked, she looked at Mrs. Langley, tears glistening in her eyes. But the old woman's smile didn't falter.

"To make magic, it takes magic." Mrs. Langley explained coolly, circling behind her. "And magic roses require magic mulch."

Suddenly, Callie felt a sharp pain sinking into her palm, and she cried out. She glanced down at her open hands and saw the beating, fluttering rosebud had now divided into two, exposing rows of ferocious teeth. The rosebud had bitten deep into her scraped-up palm and was now sucking fiercely, extracting the ruby-red blood gushing from the center. Callie screamed, both at the pain of being bitten and at the sensation of Mrs. Langley's spindly hands twisting the ends of her hair. The rosebushes trembled ferociously, their leaves rustling violently; ever so eager for their next meal. Each of the rosebuds opened to reveal their glistening teeth, and the greedy grasses climbed even higher up Callie's legs. Mrs. Langley pushed her forward, and the girl tumbled head over heels into the many open, hungry mouths of the beasts.

CHLOE SPENCER *is an award-winning author, game developer, and filmmaker whose work has been seen in numerous publications, including* Kotaku, GameLuster, *and* TechRadar. *Her debut sci-fi romance novel,* Duality, *recently received a finalist award in the Lesfic Bard competition. You can find more of her work at chloespenceronline.com.*

RAGE

Rose Taylor

You could trace it now, if you were so inclined. Find the places that used to be libraries, find the things that used to be newspapers or the flickering emptiness of what were once websites; scroll back and back and say, "ah, yes, here is where it started. And here and here and here, all those stories lost like the horizon at nightfall, these were where it started."

Except...

You have no interest in that. You curl yourself, long legged and awkward, around a fire, and you watch. There are others with you of course, no-one goes out alone now, but the others watch you.

You became the leader in the same way you slipped your name, unwilling, unwanting. A fact that you cannot argue with, and they watch you for guidance, safety, reassurance, under the darkness that was a functioning country a year ago.

"I heard something," someone says. They drag a flare across onto their lap; you say nothing. The world is full of ghosts now, and many of them are noisy.

"Are you sure?" someone else says.

You're sure that water still runs downhill, but everything else is still in flux. A noise could be anything or nothing, and at least half of them are born of nightmares that haunt people into the waking world.

"Maybe... there, look!"

You've been staring at the fire for too long. Reds and yellows dance in front of your eyes, a banner raised in defence of humanity against the everything else, and it blinds you as you stare.

Something moves, heartbeat quick, between the trees.

You squint, try to chase the ghosts of the flames away.

Many headed, or is it just many of them, pressed close together in their fear?

You raise a hand.

Breathe and wait and listen and feel the memories of an office chair, the curve of a mouse in your hand, as you look across the field. You didn't know you'd end up here. No-one did.

It's deer. They shatter out from the herd, shrapnel of brown fur and dark, wild eyes.

"Don't let them get too close," you say, as though anyone needs to hear it. Perhaps it's a defiance thing; a "we are a human and we will use our voices even at the end" thing. You've been thinking about that a lot lately.

If you're thinking, you're not one of those things stumbling half broken in their own circle of Hell, trying to drag the rest of the world down with them.

"Now!" you bark, and the flares blaze, the lights blind.

Deer cannot scream. You knew that before. Dogs can, and horses, and parrots, of course, but not deer. If anyone still studied philosophy, there'd be a study to be done in the ethics of anything that gave nature half a voice but only allowed it to be used to scream.

So many things scream now. Maybe that's the worst of it.

Light sensitive. The water phobia pulled back, the foaming lasts a lot longer than it should, the rage isn't so much a driver anymore, but then, it doesn't need to be, not if it's airborne.

Seems like half the world is rabid now. Whatever didn't get shot or cut down in the first wave is, at least, and then anything that they can breathe on.

You watch the deer scatter, still screaming.

Or maybe you're going mad and it's different screams you're hearing.

You watch them fade away.

You remember stories that coalesced in a couple of weeks in a long, hot summer. Stories that came from far away, from hunters and farmers and ranchers and other people who didn't seem to matter to the glossy, real, world. They're not the ones you could research, because no-one wrote those down, but people have found each other in the woods and the mountains and the wilds and brought the first stories with them.

The cattle that turned in an abattoir and trampled the slaughtermen, broke through their pens and shambled out in blood-stained herds.

The family dog, loyal and gentle, until... You don't need the until, you know what comes next. It was quick and violent and repeated across the world.

The birds who turned away from their seed and gathered, raincloud dark, against the windows of the houses until the glass fractured under their beaks.

How it was slow at first and in other countries and it was a joke, it was a hoax, and then it was real, and you all left all the lights burning to keep the animals away, and eventually the lights started to go out, all over the world.

You have no expectation to see them lit again in your lifetime.

You wonder, still, if someone else made the same connections as you. How those things seemed to have with intelligence, with direction; with fury and hunger and terror all mixed in but always under direction.

Can a virus bring intelligence along with it? Forethought and planning and a desire to harm?

Is it rabies or is it rage?

You don't know.

A bird shrieks above. A hoof stamps in the distance. Something moves in the pool, ripples in the moonlight, and you are only a human, surrounded by nature, and you are so very, very afraid.

ROSE TAYLOR is an occasional author living in the UK. They currently work with rescue horses and enjoy reading and writing fantasy and horror. They haven't met any possessed animals... yet.

THE BLUE MOSS HEART

Nico Bell

Layla had one chance. She stared across the prison table and into Jackson's amused expression. He winked and chuckled.

Layla kept her composure as she set the small voice recorder on the table and gave it a little push toward him. "Tell me about your burns."

Jackson shrugged and leaned back in his chair. "Not much to say. When I took Her heart from Her body, it burned me. I imagine you've read all about it. Shit, you probably know more about my burnt-up hands then I do. No one will show me the medical report. Some doctor bandaged them up, and that's about it." He held up his wrapped hands covered in dirty blood-stained gauze. "I guess they figure I don't need to have them cleaned, or the Band-Aids cleaned. You know, since I'm gonna die soon anyways."

"So, it's true? Your cancer has spread?"

"You know it has or else you wouldn't be here." He smirked. "But I'll tell you the same thing I've told all the other reporters." He learned a little closer. The air between them thickened with the stench of nicotine and arrogance. "I'm not telling you where I put Her heart."

Perspiration beaded on Layla's upper lip. A tiny window near the top of the cell allowed the sun's rays to shine through. Even indoors with the air conditioners on full blast, the heat burnt her pale skin and sweat slicked her palms.

"I honestly didn't think I'd live long enough to see the side effects of everything I've done."

Layla's jaw twitched. "So, you were just going to destroy the environment, melt the world, and then quietly slink off into your mansion and die?"

He shrugged. "It doesn't really matter now."

"You could fix all of this." Layla hated the small plea in her voice, but she didn't have time to play around. "Tell me where Her heart is so I can heal our world."

Jackson stared out the window. "Has anyone told you about it? Her heart, I mean. Did someone brief you on it?"

Layla took a deep breath. "Please, our planet is running out of time."

"It's covered in blue moss." A small smile tugged at his lips. "Can you believe that? Just the most calm and quiet shade of blue."

"Jackson," Layla rested her elbows on the table. "Why won't you tell someone where it is?"

"Because we don't deserve it." He looked back at her with a sense of sadness. "I've had plenty of time to sit here and think, and I've seen the error of my ways even if no one else on this damn planet does. Everyone says that I killed Her, but I didn't. Mother Nature wanted to die. She let me do it."

"No." Layla shook her head. "You're just trying to distract me. You have the solution to help us, and you're being an asshole about it."

Jackson chuckled without humor. "Sweet talkin' me won't help."

"So, that's it? We just sit around and wait for the Earth to overheat and the oceans to dry up and the animals to die and all of us to wither away and become extinct."

"That will only be the end of *our* story. That's what She showed me. She was as close to me as I am to you, and She showed me what would come next, and it's so much more worthy and beautiful."

Layla got up and started pacing. "You're crazy."

"I ended *this* world, not *the* world, but She forgave me and gave me the responsibility to make sure it burns to the ground so—"

"Yeah, I know. Something better can take our places." But Layla refused to accept it. Jackson may have been done living, but she wasn't. Her mind ticked away, replaying everything he'd said. "Blue moss." She froze. "Mother Nature's heart is made of blue moss."

She smiled and grabbed the voice recorder.

"No!" He stood, but his shackles made it impossible for him to stop her.

Layla banged on the door and a second later, a guard opened it.

"You can't go against Her!"

She ignored him and hurried out of the jail, into the bright sunlight. Layla cursed at the humidity that smacked her cheeks.

There weren't many stretches of green still thriving in the city. With the climate changes and the radical weather over the years, things started to die and never come back, but there was one place that still sprouted new patches of grass, one place that was still maintained and honored and revered.

Layla pulled up to the cemetery. She took a calming breath to try and settle her racing pulse as she began walking down the row to the largest tree centered amongst the gravestones.

It still bloomed green leaves that provided respite from the sun. The tree had a nook carved into the lower side, and when she kneeled to look inside, her pulse almost stopped.

There, resting in the dark hole, was Mother Nature's blue moss heart.

"Holy crap."

This was what she'd been searching for ever since Jackson's face became a news staple. This was her ticket to restarting the Earth, to a greener future, to a Pulitzer and her smiling image on the front of every news site in the world.

Layla laughed and let the moment sink in. She'd saved the world.

She showed me what would come next, and it's so much more worthy and beautiful.

Screw that. Humanity deserved another chance.

She started to dig. The ground was dry and hard as she clawed her way down. The dirt tickled her nostrils, but she kept going until a little hole was made. With trembling hands, she reached into the tree nook and cradled the heart. The moss was soft and cool to the touch, and as she pulled it from its hiding place, the blue grew rich and dark and turned a deep shade that reminded her of the ocean. Not the actual ocean. That was currently filled with plastic. No, it reminded her of the pictures of the sea she'd studied in textbooks.

Layla placed the heart into the hole. Slowly, she covered it with the dirt and patted the spot flat.

You can't go against Her.

She shook her head. Mother Nature got it wrong. Thankfully, Layla fixed it.

A breeze began to twirl around the tree. Layla stood and smiled as the temperature cooled.

"It's working." She laughed. "It's actually working."

She stepped out from the tree's shade, and her skin didn't burn under the heat of the sun. The wind picked up and whipped her hair and sent goosebumps down her arm as the temperature continued to cool. A cloud appeared—had it been there before? It didn't matter. It was here now, like a gallant knight sent to battle the sun. A second later, it covered the harsh yellow light, and for the first time in a very long time, Layla shivered. She smiled and rubbed her hands over her arms to keep them warm as the cloud turned gray and then black. It started to rain, a little at first, and then all at once.

Layla raised her hands up to the sky and let the water drip from her body.

Then, she spotted the twister just over the ridge.

"No." The joy drained from her body as the funnel rotated quicker, collecting speed and debris. Thunder roared and lightening crackled to the ground causing the ground to sizzle beneath her feet. She yelped and started running to her car.

"No, no, no." She'd done everything right. She'd gotten Jackson to give up information, she'd figured out where the heart was, she'd put it back in the Earth… Everything should be fixed, not getting worse.

There was something in front of her car. No, not something. Someone.

Her feet stumbled to a stop.

Mother Nature stood in her path, a human shape constructed with interwoven vines, dotted with lilies and roses and irises, a mix of white and pink and purple. Moss filled the spots between the flowers, and if it weren't for the way Her daisy eyes narrowed and bore into Layla, She would have looked peaceful.

"We…we can fix it." Layla's hair whipped in the growing storm. "Please, let us have another chance."

"Enough chances." Mother Nature's voice was soft, but stern. She raised her hand into the air and another twister began to form on the horizon. And another, and another.

"Oh, God. Please." Layla dropped to her knees.

But the time for pleading and fixing had passed. The time for second and third and fourth chances was over. The time for humanity had come to an end, and the time for something better, more deserving to take its place, had begun. Layla knew all of this, felt all of this, and she wept until the final moments.

Mother Nature had enough. The end had come.

NICO BELL is the author of horror novella Food Fright *and the editor of horror anthology* Shiver. *She's had several short stories published in both horror and romance. She can be found at www.nicobellfiction.com and on Twitter and Instagram @nicobellfiction.*

ACKNOWLEDGEMENTS

Thank you, as always, to all the authors who sent in their wonderful stories and poetry. This one was a particularly tough call, and a lot of excellent pieces unfortunately didn't make it in. Flash fiction is an awkward length, and I have the greatest of respect for everyone who took up the challenge!

Thanks also to all our Patrons and supporters, and everyone who goes out of their way to share the word and promote our books. You guys are all amazing.

Much love,

Antonia

ALSO AVAILABLE FROM GHOST ORCHID PRESS

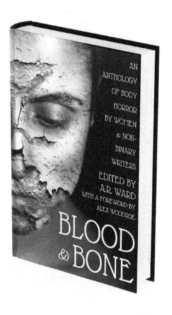

Blood & Bone: An Anthology of Body Horror by Women & Non-Binary Writers

ghostorchidpress.com